the bird room

chris killen

CANONGATE
Edinburgh · London · New York · Melbourne

First published in Great Britain in 2009 by
Canongate Books Ltd, 14 High Street,
Edinburgh EH1 1TE

1

The epigraph is from *The Temple of the Golden Pavilion* by Yukio Mishima, published by Secker & Warburg. Reprinted by permission of the Random House Group

British Library Cataloguing-in-Publication Data
A catalogue record for this book is available on
request from the British Library

ISBN 978 1 84767 260 5

Typeset by Cluny Sheeler

Printed and bound in Great Britain by Clays Ltd, St Ives plc

www.meetatthegate.com

At the same time as looking, I must subject myself to being thoroughly looked at.

Yukio Mishima, *The Temple of the Golden Pavilion*

I am not a man. I am a hat stand.

I'm standing in the corner of the living room, naked. Her favourite hat hangs from my erection. It's getting cold. I've been here too long.

Oh god, I should start again somewhere else.

Paintings of small birds. Wrens, robins, chaffinches, budgies (lots of budgies), birds like that. All bright yellows, reds, browns and greens, except for the pigeon. The pigeon is grey.

I'm on the sofa. She's sitting next to me. She has her legs crossed. There's about this much space between us. Will's in the kitchen, making cups of tea. This is the first time they've met. It is my idea.

'This is Will,' I say.

He's stood at the front door in his dressing gown. Late afternoon. The dressing gown is speckled with paint and fag ash.

'Hello, Will,' she says.

'Hello,' he says.

'Will, this is Alice.'

He invites us in and we follow him down the hall and sit in the living room. Will disappears into the kitchen. After a while we hear the rising bubble of a kettle. We aren't speaking. She's busy looking at the paintings. I've seen them before.

'How was your holiday?' I shout.

I shout it a bit too loudly.

How was your holiday? hangs in the air. It becomes louder than the kettle. We sit on the sofa listening to it. She has her legs crossed. They're crossed away from me. How was your holiday? becomes unbearably, excruciatingly loud. If all the birds in all these paintings began to sing, suddenly, they would still not be louder than How was your holiday?

I want to say something else, anything at all. I can think of nothing to say. Alice doesn't help me out. She thinks How was your holiday? is funny.

Eventually Will comes back in with the three teas – his and hers in one hand, mine in the other. He's so tall he has to stoop as he enters.

'Sorry, did you say something?' he says, handing me my mug.

I can't bring myself to repeat it.

'How was your holiday?' she asks.

I want to pour the boiling tea over myself. I want to pour it over my head and my crotch.

'Yeah, it was alright,' he says. 'Got a bit weird at the end though.'

He doesn't elaborate. He waits for us to ask. He's talking to her really. I'm just listening. Eavesdropping. And now he's looking her over, probably wondering what her tits look like. He doesn't know she has big nipples. He doesn't know she has a big nipple complex.

'How d'you mean?' she asks.

'I'll show you.'

He gets up and starts searching around in a drawer. When he comes back he sits next to her on the sofa, so the three of us are pressed up in a row. There's almost no space between us now. Only a half-millimetre of nylon and denim separates the flesh of her knee from the flesh of my knee.

I take a sip of tea. It burns my tongue.

Will is holding a stack of photographs.

'Okay,' he says. 'So I go on holiday the other week to France. I've got this friend, Clare, who's just set up this exhibition space in Paris, and I was invited out for the opening night. There was performances, free wine, all that shit.

'So, everything's going great. I'm pissed three days straight, and everywhere you look there's these beautiful French women wanting to talk about art. And it's good business, too. You know, talk shit to the right people, try and get 'em interested in my stuff . . .'

I can't believe how intently she's listening to him. She's nodding and uh-huh-ing in all the right places.

'And the weather's fucking *great*. You know how it's

been over here – pissing it down. I'd forgotten my digital camera, so I pick up this cheapie disposable thing from a newsagent.'

He passes her the first photo. She cranes over it, obscuring my view. Finally she passes it across. A picture of Will stood next to the Arc de Triomphe. He's wearing shorts and he has his hair tied back and he's grinning. He passes her another. The view from the top. Will's head pokes out from the bottom left corner. And another. Will with his arm round some bloke in a foreign football shirt. They're sat at a patio table, drinking Kronenbourgs, cheers-ing.

And another.

In 2007, Will was listed as 'one of the year's most promising artists' by a well-known magazine.

And another.

He still thinks Metallica is the best band ever.

'Anyway, once the party's over, I don't want to come back home. I decide to extend my ticket, buy one of those rail passes, you know, just sort of bum around France for an extra week and see a bit of the countryside.'

The next few are views from the train. A run of photos taken in the train's toilet. One of the toilet bowl. One of himself in the mirror. She spends an extra few seconds on that one. She knows he's an artist and she wants to impress him, so she says, 'I really like this part here, how the flash sort of bounces off the mirror. Was that intentional?'

They are very bad photographs. Will is not a photographer. He's a painter. His paintings themselves are crude, almost childish in design.

'Dunno,' he shrugs. 'Didn't really think too much about it. I was just trying to . . . capture the moment. I guess I wanted some of me in there, cuz once you're travelling by yourself it's like the whole thing's a dream. And unless you get some proof of it . . .'

He tails off. He takes the photo out of her hand. He looks at it for a long time.

'I think I wanted proof that I was there.'

I take another sip of my tea. It's gone cold. I stand it near my foot. Later, when we get up to leave, I will knock it over. I will apologise. Will will tell me it really doesn't matter. Alice will look at me like I'm a prick. I will go over the top and offer to buy him some carpet shampoo. She will say, 'Fuck's sake, it's just tea. It's not *blood*.'

'So I end up at the coast, at this beach. God knows where. I book into a little guesthouse and there's none of the usual tourist shit around for miles. It's really quiet and I'm having a whale of a time – on the beach every day, smoking Gauloises, having a read. I even buy myself some trunks, to go swimming in the sea.'

I can't see where this is going. I'm waiting for the point and doubting there is one. Maybe this is nothing more than some sort of dodgy courtship ritual. I wonder if she's even listening to him or whether she's already off ticking mental boxes:

- ☐ Would he be a good fuck?
- ☐ Would he be faithful?
- ☐ Would he give me space?
- ☐ Would he do as I ask?

She passes me one of the beach. Blue waves. White sand. A bird, frozen in the sky, angled towards the sea.

There is only one photo left in his hand.

'So it's my last day before I need to get back on the train and I want a photo of myself on the beach. But there's no one around to ask, no couples or families or anything. It's a ghost beach. It gets to the afternoon, I've just been swimming in the sea and I'm drying myself off, and I really should be going, when along comes this old geezer walking across the sand dunes.

'I call him over. *Pardon, monsieur! Excuse moi!* And he hobbles down the slope towards me. It takes him ages. He must've been at least in his seventies. He's this local fella, with a plastic bag of groceries. *Je voudrais une photo*, I say, showing him the camera, you know, *photo*, like that, and he seems to understand. So I go and stand where I want it taken. I only have one picture left on the camera; it needs to be exactly right. So I get myself positioned with the sea behind me and I place him a couple of metres away. And just to make sure he gets it all in, I convince him to kneel down, too. I mean, I feel really bad cuz he's so . . . well, *old*, and it takes him fucking ages, but finally he manages it. So I go, *Okay, Monsieur!* and wait for him to take the picture.

'Nothing happens. He just takes his eye away from the viewfinder and mutters something to himself. He's shaking his head and sort of beckoning me towards him, so I assume, you know, he wants me a bit nearer . . . to get everything in. I take two steps forward, put my hands back on my hips and shout *Okay! Oui!*

'Again, nothing. He's shaking his head now and muttering and gesturing to me to come closer still . . .'

He stops talking.

There is only one photo left in his hand.

'So?' Alice asks. 'What happened?'

He passes it to her. She bends over it and sort of gasps. Her knee presses against mine. She hands it across.

It's a photo of Will's crotch. His orange trunks very nearly fill the frame. You can make out the black wisps of hair running down his thighs and curling upwards towards his belly. You can make out the spots of seawater clinging coldly to his trunks and tanned skin. You can make out the clear bulges of his cock and balls.

Artistically speaking, it's the best of the bunch.

We get home and Will is all she can talk about. How long have I known him? Where has he exhibited? How much do his paintings cost? I turn on the telly and she drifts out of the room.

An hour passes.

I want somehow, very quietly, to destroy myself.

I want to become invisible.

Then she calls me to the bedroom. She has the curtains closed and the lights out. It's only six o'clock.

'Lie down on the bed,' she says. Her voice is quiet. It's just the outline of a voice.

I can hear the slipping off of clothes. I can see her silhouette, over by the blue rectangle of window. This will be the first time we've had sex in a week. I lie down on the bed and shuffle out of my jeans. Outside a car drives past.

She climbs on top of me and lowers herself roughly onto me, the breath catching in her throat.

I start to think of that white beach again with the bird frozen above the sea. The cars going past are quiet waves. She smells like a cocktail with a little umbrella in it.

'Will,' she pants all of a sudden. It escapes her lips under the cover of breath.

What? I only just make it out.

'Will,' she says again. This time it's louder. It's almost a shout.

The beach has dissolved. The beach is a slug and she has poured salt all over it.

'Will,' she says.

'Will.'

'Will.'

'Will.'

'Will.'

Once it's over, we both lie there in the dark, static,

breathing heavily, and there is nothing I can say. I can't confront her about it, though that must seem the most obvious thing to do. I can't say a word without sounding crazy because my name is also Will.

Alice is at work. Alice thinks I'm at work. I'm not at work. I'm trying to guess the password to her email account. I've tried her birthday (160581), her middle name (victoria), her favourite colour (blue), her favourite film (breakfastattiffanys), her favourite band (thecure).

And so far, no luck.

I don't know what it is I'm supposed to have done. I don't know what's gone wrong but she doesn't even look me in the eyes any more. She's become as quiet and cold as something left on a windowsill. She's started wearing those long black jumpers that cover her neck and hang down past her knuckles. She's started turning her face away when I try to kiss her and speaking in clichés. She says things like, 'I'm just tired tonight' and 'I have a headache' and 'Don't worry, it's not you, it's me.'

But it is me, Alice, it must be. And I don't know what I've done.

If only she wrote a diary.

I imagine short sad emails to friends in other cities:

> I'm fine. London sounds nice. Is it really as expensive as everyone says? If you don't mind me asking, how much do you get paid an hour?

and

> I'm not really fine. I need to get out of here. I feel trapped and sick.

and

> I've been living with this bloke William and I really think I need to break it off. I know how awful it sounds but I can't just finish with him and go back to Mum's either. I don't know what to do. Things have run their course. I need a new start somewhere else and I figured if I told him I'd found a job in London . . .

The only time she's got excited recently was that afternoon she met Will.

Will.

What was it that excited her; the thing that seems to excite every girl he meets? It can't be his looks. His nose is long and crooked. His teeth are yellow from tea and nicotine. His hair is unwashed and scraggy and spotted with dandruff. It can't be his mind, either. Will's observations are surface-level, obvious things, un-thought-through. I don't think Will really cares what he's saying, as long as he's saying something.

So it must be some other thing, maybe the whatever-it-is that connects these ridiculous predictable elements of him together.

Also, Will doesn't stay inside all day with the curtains drawn, trying to hack into his girlfriend's email account. Will doesn't spend his mornings hidden under the duvet with his phone switched off.

I imagine them together.

Will and Alice.

They lick each other's faces like dogs. They tear off each other's clothes, not thinking, not worrying, not analysing their actions or considering the consequences.

I don't know what happened; when it was I started hating Will. I can remember us going to gigs, watching videos in the back room of his mum's house, getting into pubs underage. I can remember a night when we sat on a bench at the top of the town and looked down at it, and the town looked very small and pathetic, and we both decided we needed to get out of it and move to the city.

Back then we were such good friends.

'Once I bit the head off my sister's budgie for a dare.'

We're at the preview night for Will's exhibition and Will is telling his favourite anecdote; the one he tells to charm strangers. It's exactly the same each time he tells it. It has grown slick and cold as a pebble on a riverbed.

This is the story he told me, too, the first time we met. Stood in the school art room, I remember finding it funny and a bit shocking. I remember thinking, *Fucking hell.*

Then I heard the anecdote a hundred more times.

Fucking hell, I think, as he starts in on it again.

'I remember reaching in and picking him up – Bert, that's what Maddie called him, Bert. I remember picking Bert out of the cage and he was so still in my hand, like a toy. And my mates were all watching, thinking,

He's not gonna go through with this, surely? The funny thing is, I wasn't gonna go through with it. I was just going to put him in my mouth for a second, you know, to freak them out a bit.'

Alice is listening intently. She's using Will's anecdote as an opportunity to stare openly at his face.

She's finding his face attractive and mysterious.

She is watching his face like an advert for expensive food; a swarthy chocolate gateau with cream and black cherries.

(Will once told me his secret for attracting women: 'Just ignore them.')

'And then, I don't know what happened. I guess I thought, *fuck it*, and bit him in two.'

He swings his wine glass for effect, bringing it up near his mouth then pulling it away.

'*Snap!* Just like that.'

Some Merlot sloshes over the lip of the glass, becoming a drop of budgie's blood and spotting an art critic's shirt. The art critic dabs at the stain with his handkerchief but doesn't say anything.

'Of course, it tasted bloody awful. I mean, I spat the head out straight away, but there was still all this blood and feathers and shit in my mouth. But that wasn't even the worst part. You wanna know what the worst part was? The worst part was that I'm pretty sure I heard the little bastard scream inside my mouth, just before I did it. You wouldn't think birds screamed, would you? Well, this one did. I swear it on my mum's life.'

A journalist near the back of the group raises her pen.

Will purposefully ignores her for a while.

He licks an imaginary feather from his lips.

Then he looks her way and nods.

'Do you think perhaps this incident has had something of an impact on your work?' she says, gesturing with her pen at Will's exhibition, *Fucking Birds*.

Crooked rows of canvases line the gallery walls. Wrens, robins, chaffinches, budgies (lots of budgies). Each painting has an accompanying pair of headphones that plays you a looped audio track from a hardcore porno.

Will squints at her earnestly.

He stops licking his lips.

His mouth becomes a slit.

Lines appear on his forehead.

Will is thinking. You can almost hear it.

The group wait for him to speak. A whole minute passes. People start shuffling around uncomfortably. They start examining their fingernails. Even Alice looks confused. She's still staring at him, but her eyes have narrowed and switched off, which they do sometimes; they become cold and dull.

'Um,' says Will, eventually. 'How do you *mean* exactly?'

A pause. Good lord.

The little group don't know how to take this.

He's being ironic, right?

Or maybe he's being post-ironic.

Or maybe he's just being dumb.

Post-dumb.

Then, very carefully, somebody begins to laugh. Someone else joins in. And soon they're all smiling and laughing and clapping Will on the back. Good one, they're saying politely. Good one.

Will's face flickers from confusion to pretending-he-gets-it then back again.

I edge my way in through the crowd, reach out my hand and touch Alice on the shoulder. She turns to face me with those blank cold eyes.

'I'm going to have another look round,' I tell her.

'Alright,' she says, like I've just told her some irrelevant fact off the back of a matchbox.

So I go over to the free drinks by myself.

There are a lot of people here. It's a small gallery space, somewhere in London, and we've booked into a hotel for the night. We'll go back to our room later this evening in a taxi, not speaking, not touching each other, and hoping the hotel bed will be big enough and cold enough to be almost like sleeping by ourselves.

I'm not going to ask what's wrong.

She's not going to tell me.

This was her idea. When the cryptic little invitation

card fell onto the doormat – just the date, the address and a stencil of a yellow bird – it was Alice who suggested attending. It might be *fun*, she said. And her eyes sparkled. She smiled at me. Alright, I said, thinking, I should do more things like this if it will make you happy.

(But as far as I can tell, neither of us is happy.)

I look around.

I'm not having fun.

I have nothing to say to these people.

I notice a tall thin woman at the opposite end of the gallery. She is standing next to a large painting of a lurid orange-breasted robin, but facing away from it, her wine glass lost in the spindly white claw of her fingers. She's wearing a shiny red dress that hangs off her body as if it's very bored. Her long dark hair is piled up on top of her head. She's wearing a big black pair of sunglasses.

I can't stop looking at her.

Alice is probably still at the front of the group, listening.

Will's probably started in on some new anecdote by now: 'When I was a kid, I accidentally burned my nan's house down' or 'One time at uni I fucked this epileptic.'

A man walks towards the woman and touches her on the shoulder. He's tired-looking and grey-haired. He's dressed like a secondary school teacher. He whispers something in her ear and she turns to him and smiles. He takes her elbow gently in his hand. He leads her across the gallery and positions her in front of a sparrow. It's only when she puts out her hand and leaves it there –

letting him take the headphones off the wall for her and put them in her palm, her fingers anticipating them, twitching and fumbling slightly – that I realise; she's blind.

He whispers something else in her ear, touches her shoulder and goes off into the crowd.

She's put on the headphones.

She's only a few metres away from me.

I walk up behind her. The dress is cut low at the back, so you can see pockmarks, freckles and the fine down at the nape of her neck. Closer still is her scent; not perfume but something medicinal, like a long clean hospital corridor.

From where I'm standing, I can hear the whisper of porno, leaking from her headphones.

I close my eyes and breathe her in.

Later, Will takes us to Tequila Mockingbird (his favourite Mexican-themed bar).

He will not let me buy any of the drinks.

He buys round after round of beers and shooters, bringing out fistfuls of notes and coins from his pocket and dropping them onto the bar. Then he stands back, making the bartender reach over and sort through for the correct amount.

Will does not tip, either. He refuses. 'I will not tip,' he shouts in my ear and then doesn't. He just scrapes the remaining wet notes and coins off the bar and shoves the mess back into his pocket.

We're sat at a corner booth, crammed in, our knees touching under the table; just Will, Alice and me. I'm on my fourth Corona label. Alice is smiling at him. Her eyes are bright and sparkling. Will is drunkenly saying something about art (with a capital A), some half-formed thing that calls for lots of dramatic hand gestures and the slamming of his bottle on the table.

'There should be no division,' he's saying, 'between art and life. There should be no division between "high art" and "low art". In fact, there should be no division between anything and anything.'

He looks at Alice when he says this.

'All things should just be basically fucking each other at all times.'

His teeth are grey. His lips are black from all the free wine at the preview. Now his chin too is slicked wet and glittering from the beer and tequila.

'Cause that's all humankind's after, right? Hardcore fucking. Cosmic tits and ass.'

I try to speak. 'So when . . .'

But Will isn't listening to anyone except himself.

'One day,' he's saying, 'I swear I'll find a way to fuck my own cock, like some kind of Möbius strip.'

I try again. 'So when are you moving to London, Will?'

This time he hears me.

So does Alice.

I feel her flinch slightly and she stops smiling.

'Dunno,' he says. 'London's bullshit.' Then, after a pause, 'I want to live somewhere real – Norwich or fucking Preston or something. London's everything *wrong* with contemporary art.'

His eyes narrow and he turns to Alice.

'By the way,' he says, 'I've forgotten your name.'

She smiles. She actually smiles when he says this.

'It's Alice,' she says. 'Like the looking-glass.'

'And what do you do, Alice?'

'I'm in eyes.' She flutters her eyelashes. 'I work in an optician's. It's rubbish. I should quit.'

He takes her hand off the table, lifts it to his mouth and licks a drop of tequila from her fingertip.

'Well, Alice-who-works-in-eyes, you, me and William here should go out for dinner sometime. What d'you reckon?'

She doesn't even think it over.

'Yeah,' she says, nodding vigorously. 'That'd be nice. We really don't get out enough. In fact, we hardly do anything.'

I say nothing. It's settled.

There's hardly any money left. Next week the rent's due, the week after that the council tax. I've told Alice there's been some sort of mistake with my job and the people who handle the payroll are in the process of sorting it out. In the meantime, she pays for everything. She puts a bag of groceries on the kitchen table. She doesn't look me in the eyes. I want to kiss her, but if I kiss her now, she might burst into tears.

I will take out a loan.

I will extend my overdraft.

I will start selling my possessions on eBay.

Will calls the land line. Alice answers. She turns into someone else. She stands in the hall, twisting a strand of hair around her finger, biting her lip and jiggling at the knees. She laughs three times. 'That would be lovely,' she says, putting a finger to her mouth and biting at a hangnail.

'We're going out for dinner this Friday,' she tells me afterwards, 'with Will. I'll have to get something nice to wear.'

She goes into the bathroom and starts running the bath. She takes off her work clothes and lets them drop to the floor. She looks at her body in the mirror, before it steams up, and she is chalk-white, like a primed empty canvas. She waits for something wonderful to happen to her. In her head, Will appears behind her. He puts his hands on her waist, slides them up over her tits and magically her nipples harden.

I'm fucked.

I want to disappear.

I want to not be a part of things any more.

An Italian restaurant. This is Will's choice. 'The best lasagna in the city', apparently. We're still on the garlic bread. In the corner of the room a widescreen TV plays international football on mute.

Will gets up to go for a piss.

'What is it?' Alice asks me once he's gone.

'Nothing,' I say.

'Relax,' she says.

'I don't know,' I say.

'What's wrong?' she says.

I take a sip of wine and miss my mouth.

'For god's sake,' she says.

I want to start again. I want to completely start my life again; to make no mistakes this time; to somehow watch my life from behind a screen; to double-click on the options of my life, very carefully and in my own time. There will only ever be two options to choose from and they will be easy ones, things like 'go forwards' or 'go backwards'. Things like 'yes' or 'no'.

'This is great,' Will says when he gets back from the toilet, grinning so wide you can see the fillings in his back teeth.

'Yeah,' I say. 'Really great.'

I feel for Alice's foot and press down lightly on it with my own. She doesn't seem to notice so I press down harder. Still nothing, so I press down really, really hard. Then I look under the table. I'm pressing down on a curled bit of the table leg.

The food arrives.

They've both ordered lasagna.

I've punished myself with the blandest item on the menu.

'So, have I told you about my new idea?' Will says with his mouth full.

On TV the football finishes nil–nil.

I double-click on Alice in my head.

I will double-click on her until she falls in love with me again.

'What's that?' she says.

'I'm going to hire a girl,' he says.

I will copy and paste myself into the folder of her affections.

'How d'you mean?' she says. 'Like a call girl?'

Pull yourself together, I tell myself. Start having a nice time.

'Yeah,' he says. 'Kind of. I'm going to hire some girl to have a relationship with me and then break up with her and exhibit it all. I'll take photos and video and audio of everything. Absolutely everything. So when you go into the gallery, it'll be like really uncomfortable and you'll wonder how much of this stuff you should be seeing. And then . . .'

The waiter interrupts, to ask how everything is. He calls Will *seniore*. He calls Alice *seniorina*.

'*Magnifico*,' Will replies. 'Just *magnifico*.'

I excuse myself.

In the toilets I lock myself in a cubicle and get out my mobile.

I type a message:

Nothing is wrong. I love u. I love u. I'll try & sort myself out I promise. I'm sorry. X

I delete it and try again:

If you like Will so much why dont u just fucking go home w/ him tonight instead? Its over. This is ridiculous.

And then again:

If u see this msg while were still @ the restaurant & if u still love me please tap my foot with yrs 3 times.

I settle on nothing and flush the toilet instead, watching the water crash and whirl in the empty bowl.

Back at the table, they've moved on to vegetarianism.

'I was one for years,' says Will.

(This is a lie. Will was vegetarian for about three months. Even then he was the kind that still eats chicken and fish.)

Now the TV is showing footage of a heart transplant operation. Looks like I'm the only one who's noticed. Couples at the other tables gaze at each other lovingly. Families and friends clink glasses, waiters and waitresses mill about, as behind them a middle-aged man lies slumped on an operating table with his chest laid open and his heart twitching and flapping obscenely.

I stab my spaghetti.

I double-click on Will.

I select and delete him.

'Are you sure you want to send Will to the Recycle Bin?' I ask myself, then click 'Yes'.

'I guess I went veggie 'cause I started wondering what right I had to eat an animal, a rabbit or whatever. I mean, *surely I'm just being selfish?* I thought. And then I realised, you know, we're all just animals at the end of the day.'

The surgeon's knife goes in.

'And what do animals do? They eat each other. They eat each other and they fuck. You see what I'm saying?'

'I think so,' Alice says quietly.

She twirls a strand of hair around her finger.

She lets her mouth fall very slightly open.

She moistens her bottom lip seductively with her tongue.

'It's nothing to feel guilty about, is what I'm saying. It's natural. It's *nature.* If this was the wild, we'd probably be fucking by now . . . if we weren't *eating* each other, that is.'

He raises an eyebrow and she smirks.

'But we've constructed all these . . . *distractions*. Restaurants, art galleries, clothes to wear, fucking stupid television programmes to watch. If this was the wild, Alice, I'd be fucking you right now, I'm sure of it.'

Why don't you just sweep the plates off the table and climb onto it, Alice? Hike up your skirt and beg him to fuck you.

I might as well not exist.

'What about me?' I say.

'You'd probably be dead by now,' Will says, 'if this was the wild.'

'That's a bit harsh,' Alice says, smiling.

'His eyesight,' Will says. 'Think about it. He'd be picked off by a lion or something.'

When the bill comes, Will insists on paying.

I take out my wallet anyway, swearing I had more money than this, wondering where it's all gone and making a show of going through it; getting out the one ten-pound note I have left and all my bits of paper and cards and things and laying them on the table, saying, 'If you want, I can put it on my card . . .'

Will says, 'Don't be a twat. It's on me. My pleasure.'

Then I say something.

'We'll have to do this again,' I say.

What am I saying?

'You should give us a call later in the week,' I say.

'Alright,' Will says. 'I will.'

Outside he offers to sub me the cab fare home.

I tell him we're fine with the bus.

'*Magnifico*,' he says, smiling at Alice. 'Just *magnifico*.'

I sit up in bed and throw off the covers. It's early morning and I'm sweating coldly, my stomach feeling sour and twisted.

'What's up? What's going on?' Alice says, startled and half-asleep.

'Nothing,' I say. 'Shh. Shh.'

I stroke her hair and wait for her to go back to sleep then crawl out of bed and take my wallet from the back pocket of my jeans. I scurry to the bathroom, where turning on the light won't wake her up. I kneel on the tiles and empty it out; all those useless receipts and club cards and expired 10% OFF vouchers and cash cards and coins and bits of fluff from in the corners and my old student ID and the strip from a fortune cookie that reads AN OUTGOING ATTITUDE IS THE KEY TO YOUR EFFORTS and my library card and a torn-off bit of menu with half a mobile number scrawled on it. I spread them out. I paw through them, again and again and again, but it makes no difference.

The note she wrote is gone.

There's this girl on the bus with yellow hair and blue eyes.

Her name is Clair, but if you called her Clair she wouldn't answer.

Not any more.

She doesn't like Clair.

Clair reminds her of things.

When she thinks of Clair, she thinks of someone else, someone with bitten fingernails and a secret wobbling tooth at the back of their mouth. She thinks of things falling down stairs, things dangling out of bins. She thinks of a boxroom as cheap and fancy as a small iced cake.

Her name is Helen now. She's been Helen for almost a year.

Only very occasionally – when she wakes up in a strange room, next to a sleeping body that she doesn't recognise and she doesn't know what time it is or remember quite how she got there, only then, and only for a few seconds – is she still Clair.

Helen is a better name for an actress.

Helen was as simple as trying on a dress. She left Clair tangled on the dressing-room floor. She's Helen now. She's an actress. She could be Amanda, Angela or Alice if she chose. Kate, Chloe or Camille. Just not Clair, she's sick of Clair.

Clair had mousy brown hair. Helen's bleached hers yellow.

Clair had brown eyes. Helen wears contacts.

Clair worked five years in Boots. Helen makes two hundred quid in an hour and a half.

Helen's legs are stinging of piss. It's not her piss. She washed them afterwards, but they're blotched red and raw. She hopes no one can smell it. Up near the train station, this lad gets on. He swaggers down the aisle. The bus is half-empty but he sits next to her, pressing his knee against hers and grinning. He plays bad hip-hop on his phone, the words rattling from the speaker like windblown tinfoil.

Helen feels her heart beat hard and rhythmically in her chest.

She looks firmly out the window and tries to focus on something at the centre of her; something as small and hard and cold as a peach stone. She will discover this thing inside her, whatever it is, and when she does she'll never let anyone touch it; not the lad, not her mum, not even God.

Next she tries to imagine no one is sitting next to her. Just empty space in the shape of someone, a minus-person. But it's no use. She can feel him there; his wet-grass hair and razor-burnt skin, his body swelling like an aggravated spot. He reeks of Lynx and sweat and the boys' changing rooms.

He is swelling in his seat.

He is puffing out his chest.

He is about to say something, too, so she gets out her phone and dials her mum.

It rings.

It rings.

It you-have-reached-the-voicemail-service-of-s.

(Her mum is in the kitchen, her sleeves rolled up, the taps thundering into the sink. She'll call Helen back later, once they're both a bit pissed, separately, on cheap wine, and even her mum will call her Helen.)

Meanwhile, the lad is continuing to swell. He's swelling past the line that divides his seat from hers. The veins are standing out on his neck. His neck is bulging over the collar of his tracksuit. Soon he'll be on top of her.

No more lads, she thinks. Lads can screw themselves from now on.

She stands and dings the bell, pushing past his knees to get off.

Helen lives in a two-bed terrace with her friend, Corrine. Except for twice a week, Corrine is away from six in the evening till four in the morning. She works as a croupier at the casino in town, not the swanky one near the roundabout, the cheap one where the only rule of dress is NO HOLES IN YOUR CLOTHES. When Corrine is not at work, she's usually asleep or she's out drinking. They hardly ever see each other. All Helen sees is half-finished dinners on the table, stubbed out Bensons in the ashtray and usually some note like: WE NEED MILK! or PLEASE TAPE GHOST AT 9 – CHANNEL 5.

Corrine, in the flesh, is a rarity.

Helen puts on the light in the living room.

CAKE LEFT IN THE FRIDGE is taped to the TV screen.

She has a shower. The water runs down her thighs. She doesn't wash between her legs with her hands. She takes the shower off the hook and points it up at herself. It stings.

In the shower (and at other times too), Helen has a sister. The sister is witty and cruel and sarcastic – not to Helen, just to everyone else. When they're alone the sister reveals her true self and it is soft and kind, like the underside of a kitten. Helen imagines this sister soaping her back now, very gently. In return she soaps the sister's back. She's never given the sister a name; it would make her feel too sad.

Helen's room is small and damp. If there were books in here, the covers of them would curl. Helen has a picture of Ethan Hawke Blu-tacked onto the wall. She has a single bed. She has no urge to do anything. The Ethan Hawke picture sheepishly avoids her gaze.

She sits down at her desk and turns on the PC. She checks her emails.

Nothing.

She checks the site where people from her old school post information about themselves.

Nothing.

She logs in to the adult contacts site and checks her message box. Three new replies to her profile:

> [Posted from G_Saunders @ 15:07] I saw your pictures. You look just what I'm after. Do you do fetish work? Gagging, submission, humiliation in particular? I am always looking for models for new fetish videos. Good rate of pay. Couple of hours work.

and

> [Posted from FootMaster @ 16:55] I am looking for girls for trample videos. You would be willing to walk on me – bare feet, heels, trainers. No sex just trampling on my face and body and neck. Will pay £100 for full afternoon. If you wank me off with your feet I will pay £200. Mail me for photos of my face and cock.

and

> [Posted from WR @ 17:39] I would like to meet you. I will pay £500 to have sex with you and film it, but I need to see you in person first to make sure. I will pay £100 just to meet you for an hour and I would like you to tell me a story about a time when you fucked a stranger. This will be your audition.

Helen clicks 'Reply'.

Helen's mum calls back later, once they're both a bit pissed, separately, on cheap wine.

'Hello, love.'

'Hi, Mum,' says Helen.

'How was work?'

'Oh, you know,' says Helen.

Helen's mum thinks Helen's rehearsing for a play. *Romeo and Juliet*, at some repertory theatre in the city. The play's been in rehearsal now for quite some time, for something approaching six months. In conversations with her mum, Helen has created a camp neurotic director, a heart-throb leading man, a sulky fingernail-biting leading lady and a bunch of alcoholic boorish set designers and minor cast members. Helen is setting up disaster, very slowly, in these conversations – cancelled rehearsals, differences of opinion, etcetera, etcetera – so that when she finally tells her mum the play's been cancelled, her mum won't be too surprised or disappointed.

'I'm *Helen* now, mum,' she told her once, for the last time, one afternoon when they were floating around Primark, fingering the blouses. 'I'm a professional actress.'

'Okay,' Helen's mum said. 'Helen.'

It felt good to hear her say it, finally. It felt scary and complete, like triumph and like standing at the top of a massive cliff.

Helen went into a dressing room and looked at herself in the mirror. She said 'Helen, Helen, Helen' in her head. She bit her tongue, tried on a dress and quietly burst into tears.

Sometimes – like when she's standing in a long queue at the Tesco Express and shuffling her basket forward with her feet – Helen feels cobbled-together. She feels like a rack of gaudy blouses and T-shirts in the Barnardo's charity shop. She looks at other people in the basket queue and wonders if they feel the same way. She wonders if their lives make sense. Sometimes she tries to make a list out of herself.

Helen eats fish-finger sandwiches at least three times a week.

She's never learned to swim.

She feels really beautiful only when she has sex with someone and then only sometimes, and then only while it's happening.

Helen thinks of herself as an actress, a proper one. Not a model and definitely not a porno one.

When she was still Clair she never finished her GCSEs, but that doesn't mean she's stupid.

I am the one in control, she tells herself. When filming a scene – when she is the thing being filmed – she imagines herself as a cog. Sometimes it's the cog in her auntie's cuckoo clock. She is turning. She is responsible for making the wooden cuckoo pop out through his wooden doors once an hour; she is responsible for making him chirp.

Helen listens to pop music on the bubble radio in the kitchen. She's never yet heard a song that means something to her. She really likes the idea of the radio, though / all that infinite variety / the tuning dial / the one wonderful song she will eventually happen on / what will happen when she does.

Helen's first sexual experience was at eleven years old with a candle. Her mum and dad were watching telly downstairs. It was turned up loud enough to carry through the floorboards. They were laughing and people on telly were laughing too. It was a funny programme. The candle didn't have a name. It was clammy in her fingers. She hid herself under the covers, shivering and hot, and became the flame on the end of it.

Duncan tried it on with her in his car, just before the shoot. Duncan sometimes finds her work. Helen is trying to find her own work, too, but it was Duncan who got her into it. He had this mate who worked for a website. He knew people. She met him in a pub.

Duncan was sweating at the neck.

He was stubbing his fag out.

He was smelling like a pickled onion.

He was smiling at her.

When you unscrew the lid of a jar of pickled onions and put your fingers inside, you are the one reaching for the onion. But when Helen opened the door to Duncan's car, the onion was the one reaching for her. It was reaching for her leg with a bloated red hand – for her left leg, right up near the crotch.

Helen didn't know what to do. Duncan had never tried it on with her before. She really needed a lift to the shoot. She didn't know where it was on her own.

So Helen closed her eyes and imagined her sister was in the car with them.

'Get the fuck off her,' the sister said, 'you fucking pickled onion. This isn't a chip shop, mate.'

It would've made Helen laugh, under different circumstances.

Duncan moved his hand up and down her leg. She could hear him breathing heavily. She could hear the breath hissing between his thick chapped lips and bad teeth. When the hand moved to her crotch, Helen grabbed it at the wrist. The hand became limp. She let go of the wrist and the hand moved away.

Helen opened her eyes.

The hand was on the steering wheel now. Duncan was looking sheepish. He was looking sheepish out the window. He mumbled 'Sorry' or something and then drove them to the shoot. Outside the house, he tried to turn himself back into a nice guy by asking Helen if she wanted him to wait for her, to give her a lift back afterwards.

Helen said no, she'd be alright with the bus.

Once Duncan was gone, Helen swore to herself never to get in a car with Duncan again. Fucking pickled onion. She'd find her own work from now on. The sister agreed this was a good idea.

A small terraced house, like the first result on a Google image search for 'English suburbia'. Helen passes a cat on her way to the door, an oil-stained moggy, creeping out from under a Ford Escort. The sister stops to stroke it, getting oil on her fingers, and is still there saying something to it when the door opens.

A squat little man in a woollen jumper and a sagging pair of trousers says, 'You must be Helen,' and ushers her in. His beard and fingers are nicotine-yellowed. Helen goes into the hall. She looks back for the sister but the sister is gone. She does that sometimes; she disappears.

The man with the beard takes Helen to a room upstairs, one with plastic sheeting taped to the floor and a cheap-looking camcorder on a tripod in the middle. Things are laid out on a little coffee table; a vibrator, a tub of jelly, some 'Chinese love beads' and an empty plastic washbasin. The man assures Helen that he has 'connections in Germany', that that's where the tape is going, that no one over here will see it.

Then he gives her the two hundred quid up-front and offers to take her coat.

'Right. Let's get to it, eh?' he says.

Helen is not even slightly asleep when she hears the voices.

They are whispering. The front door has just slammed. It's five or so in the morning. Helen has the lights off. She's been lying in her bed, on her back, trying her hardest to get to sleep by focusing on her nostrils and the air going in and out of them. She read this somewhere. She is trying to focus on one nostril at a time, isolating them in turn.

(One of the voices is Corrine's.)

The air goes *whewww*, in through one nostril.

(The other is a strange man's.)

The air goes *whewww*, out through the other.

'Darren, fuck me.'

Helen is awake. Her nostril-meditation has gone square out the window.

Helen lies as still as she can. She pictures Darren as a black guy, she doesn't know why. Tall and well-dressed. He is still wearing most of his clothes as he has sex with Corrine and his breathing makes it through the wall and into Helen's ears.

Darren's breathing is deep and raspy like the guiro in the school music room.

Corrine's is high and papery like home-made Christmas lanterns.

They aren't using the bed, Helen imagines. They're up against the wall. Corrine has her legs wrapped round Darren's back. Darren still has all his clothes on. Just his flies and his belt are undone.

Then there is a pause.

As she waits for more noises, Helen imagines how they met, with herself as Corrine: *I was working on the blackjack table. It was getting on for three when this bloke sits down. It's a quiet night – pretty much dead, only a couple of regulars playing – and then he turns up, plays a hundred quid and quickly loses it all. He has nice eyes, dark and black. He's dressed well, too – a suit and shirt and this little gold chain that I can see beneath his collar. He brings out a big wad of twenties and cashes another hundred and loses that, too. I have to be very professional not to laugh at him. He doesn't even win one hand. It's quite sad, really, and he seems serious, as if he's coming in here to lose on purpose – like this is a special game he's playing and one win will screw it all up. Maybe he is, I think. I can't stop looking at his hands, either. He has such long neat perfect fingers.*

The guiro and Christmas lanterns resume their scraping and fluttering.

He doesn't look at me again, apart from that first time, and I really want him to. I'm breathing heavier and sticking my tits out, hoping he'll look at them. We have to wear such horrible blouses in here and I hope he doesn't think I'm ugly. I start making jokes with the regulars in the hope that he'll laugh too, but he doesn't. When he cashes a third hundred his hand touches mine. We aren't supposed to touch the customers, ever, but I don't say anything. It only happens for a second and I get wet just from him touching my hand.

They are louder now. It sounds like Christmas morning in the school music room. The lanterns are going fuck, fuck, fuck over and over again.

Then – all of a sudden – he gets up and leaves. I watch him walk out the door and my heart sinks. It's gone three and I don't finish till four. At the end of my shift I check out, get my stuff and as I'm standing outside waiting for my taxi I feel this big warm hand on my shoulder. I turn round and it's him. He's been waiting for me all this time. And we don't even say anything then, we both just wait and get into my taxi when it arrives. In the back of the cab, he puts his hands on me and whispers in my ear and I melt.

The noises have stopped. Helen is lying in her bed, her heart hammering hard. Something is caught in her throat. She's excited and scared. She's just had a very good idea.

This is the thing I'll tell him, she thinks. This is the story I will tell WR.

It turned out the real Darren – the one who slunk down the stairs behind Corrine, as Helen was halfway through lunchtime *Neighbours* – was some bulldog white bloke with shit tattoos and sovereign rings and a thick pink neck like uncooked sausage skin.

This is fine.

Helen's Darren is tucked away safely inside her. She's polished him up a bit, added things to him. And later she will ask Corrine a list of questions about the casino – little details to make it sound more plausible – because research is what good actresses do.

Corrine said her and Darren were going out for lunch. She told Helen she wouldn't be home before work.

Helen's in Corrine's room.

She's lying in Corrine's bed, pulling the covers around her, sniffing in the musky smell of their post-sex bodies. She's dressed in Corrine's spare casino uniform and seeing herself from above, like some kind of glamorous Hollywood suicide crime scene photograph; tranquillisers, champagne, her make-up immaculate.

Helen has all the windows open. Maybe this will cure the damp, somehow. It is raining and freezing, and the curtains of Corrine's room flutter, like there are men behind them; Tom Selleck, Ethan Hawke and Chandler from *Friends.* They watch Helen curl and uncurl, swishing her legs in Corrine's bed. They have their big celebrity hands down their trousers.

Helen follows a stream of middle-aged middle-class men and women off the bus. She's at the very edge of the city now, the nicer part of town. Victorian townhouses. BMWs. It's still raining here, but only very lightly. Streets like this look nice in the rain. The pavements are dark. They reflect the just-gone-on streetlamps. Helen has the address written down on the back of an envelope. She holds it in her hand. Her hand shakes. She isn't nervous. She isn't nervous. Two weeks ago shc pissed into a brandy glass. She filled it to the brim, in front of a cameraman and a soundman and this bloke who just watched who said he was the producer. She wanked herself off with a shoe. She shouldn't be nervous.

Helen is stood outside his house.

No BMW in the drive.

The front garden is overgrown.

Something – a skirt? – is tangled in the bushes.

She has to step round snails and slugs to get to the front door. The curtains are drawn. Her finger hovers over the doorbell. She rests the tip of her finger on it and takes a deep breath.

And then her phone goes off. It startles her. She snatches it out of her raincoat pocket. She takes a few steps back down the drive, putting some distance between her and the door, and treads on a snail accidentally. She checks the display. It's her mum.

Helen waits for the phone to stop ringing. She holds it in her hands, waiting for her mum to put down the receiver. She thinks about lighting a fag but decides against it. Once the phone stops ringing, she steps carefully back past the snails.

This time the door opens before she can touch the bell.

'Are you Helen?' says the man in the doorway, extending his hand towards her.

She nods.

'I'm William,' he says. 'Or Will.'

His hand is cold. She forces a smile. He doesn't. His face is drawn and dark with stubble. She's guessing he's thirty but it's pretty hard to tell. There's this blankness to him, as if he's more an idea than an actual person.

Something is missing.

William or Will shakes her hand for a long time, long enough for the coldness of it to go in through her fingers and start to make its way up her arm like tetanus.

Then he turns and leads Helen inside.

If the phone rings again I'll unplug it. I'll throw it away.

I've quit my job.

I've quit my job by not going in.

Wednesday morning, 10 a.m. The phone's rung three times already today; the answerphone is at its message limit.

One from my parents, from four days ago: 'Hello, William, mum and dad here. Just a quick call to see if you're okay. Give us a ring when you get this, love.'

One from Will, two days ago: 'Got back from Prague last night. It was bollocks. Anyway, give me a call. There's someone I'd like you to meet.'

The other forty-eight are from my boss.

I've not told anyone yet, but I plan to work from home from now on, for myself. I've got the necessary 'start-up capital' saved in the bank. My new job will involve sitting around watching TV and eating toast and not going to work any more. It will involve looking out of the window and daydreaming and avoiding people from work.

Further than this, I don't know.

I have nothing planned.

I lie in bed, not picking up the phone and imagining someone; a girl I've not yet met. This afternoon she'll knock on my door. Her knock will be distinctive; sharp and very slightly brittle. Just hearing the knock I'll know it's her. I'll smooth down my hair in the bathroom mirror. I'll take my time over it, too, because she is patient and will wait on the doorstep for as long as it takes. (She will wait an hour if she has to.) Then I'll invite her in and we'll sit in the living room, talking about small quiet things for a while and drinking cups of tea. We'll make jokes. We'll understand each other immediately. We'll understand things we previously didn't even know existed. Then she'll move in. This will all happen in the same afternoon. It will happen today. And nothing will be difficult between us, nothing will need to be arranged, because from now on there'll be no supermarkets, bosses, gas or electricity bills ever again. Carpet warehouses, solicitors, tax return forms – such things won't exist any more. Every boring and depressing part of our lives – even those crouched on its periphery, like the dull brown buildings you see zip past on the bus – will be eradicated.

She will be kind and quiet and sweet.

She will fall in love with me, completely and suddenly.

We will stay in bed all day with the curtains drawn and not get up, even if we really need to piss.

I arrange to meet Will at a bar in the city. A few years ago, we'd be out for a drink every other night. Now I hardly see him. He has other friends – 'art friends', 'contacts' – these days.

Walking in, it wasn't yet dark and I felt shifty and awkward. I pulled up the hood of my coat. I expected to turn a corner and run into Peter from work or Simon or Clare or Allan. I expected to run into some wrong-turn of conversation, leading to why I'd not been in and how I'd been 'under the weather' or 'not feeling up to things, recently', and what's been going on in the office, and when I'll be back, etcetera.

I'd shuffle around and look at the floor and lie at them until they'd gone.

Or worse, my boss. Prowling the streets, with my number set to speed dial.

I'll not get a reference now.

I get there late. Will's sat in a booth at the back. He's opposite a girl. They're holding hands across the table. When he sees me, he waves. She turns round in her seat. She's blonde. Her face is pointed and flickering in the candlelight. She looks nice. She smiles at me.

Will gets up. We shake hands. With his free hand he claps me on the back. He has stolen this gesture from somewhere; I've not seen it before. His grip is strong, like someone's dad's. One of my fingers pops loudly at the knuckle.

Will tries out new personality traits.

I don't think he knows he's even doing it.

For a few months last year he took to holding cigarettes between the second and third fingers of his left hand.

'William, this is Katrina.'

'Hello,' she says to me, sounding shy, possibly East-European.

She's very pretty. Smooth skin, straight hair, her eyes a greeny-blue colour.

'And Katrina, this is my good friend, William.'

I curl my mouth into a smiling shape. I nod my head as if I'm agreeing with something. Katrina. I have nothing to say.

'Sit down, sit down,' he says. 'I'll get the drinks.'

He leaves us alone.

I pull up a chair and wait for her to say the first thing.

The next table over, someone starts telling a long involved joke.

'So . . .' says Katrina. 'Will doesn't tell me what you do.'

I look over. Leant across the bar, he's saying something directly into the barman's ear, his shirt hanging out from under his jacket. If I dressed like that, I'd just look a mess. But somehow Will makes himself look stylishly dishevelled; purposefully 'artistic'. I wonder if he spends time in front of the mirror messing up his clothes and buttoning his shirt in the wrong holes.

'I'm . . . unemployed,' I say.

'Oh,' says Katrina.

'I just quit my job.'

The joke reaches its punch line and the people at the next table begin to laugh.

'You quit your job?'

'Yep.'

'Why?'

Will sits back down. He puts a pint of lager in front of me. For him and Katrina, a second bottle of red wine. He starts to refill their glasses.

'I was just telling Katrina here that I quit my job.'

Will stops pouring the wine and stands the bottle on the table.

'You quit your job?'

'Yep.'

'Why?'

I take a big swig of my pint. On the walk over, I was planning on telling him some sort of elaborate lie. But instead I decide on the truth. I begin to tell him – to tell them both – how trapped and panicked I was feeling. About how sometimes I would go into cold sweats at the bus stop. How I have a bit of money saved up and how I don't feel like I can fill out one more monotonous form or enter another ream of data into a spreadsheet or type up another six-page report for a very long time. I tell them I plan to reduce the things in my life, to find the small essential elements in it and just focus on those for a while. Finally, I tell them – as clichéd as it sounds – that I want to 'start again from scratch'.

Will gets excited. He says it sounds like something this artist, Tehching Hsieh, might do. He attempts to turn my decision into a piece of performance art and says I should document everything, keep a journal and take a photo of myself once a day.

He's a bit drunk. He's showing off to Katrina.

She listens quietly, her eyes lowered, fingering the stem of her wine glass.

Later, when she's gone to the toilet, he leans across the table and whispers in my ear, 'I met her on the bus back from the airport. It's her first time in England. She's supposed to be staying with her cousin, but she spent last night at mine.'

'Great,' I say.

'Not really. I might finish with her tonight. She doesn't talk that much and she's rubbish in bed.'

Out in the street, Will hails a taxi. We're all a bit drunk. He ushers Katrina into it, then beckons to me, offering me a lift home. I tell him I'll walk.

I stop for chips somewhere.

I weave through the city centre, past groups of men 100x more pissed and violent than I am.

I should go straight home, get into bed, pull the covers over my head and try to dream about that girl I'll meet.

But instead, I join the queue to a nightclub.

The swing of the cab presses her close against me. It straightens from the turn but she doesn't pull away. Her hand gropes for mine. She leans into me, heavy and vodka-smelling.

'I don't normally do this,' she says.

'Do what?'

'Go home with strange men in taxis.'

'Me neither.'

'You're not strange, are you?' she says into my coat.

'I don't think so.'

'Good,' she says. 'I need to be looked after.' She says this last bit abstractedly, almost to herself.

She leans her head on my shoulder and closes her eyes. I think she's gone to sleep, but then her hand untangles itself. It moves onto my thigh. Her head shifts from my shoulder. She bites my arm through my sleeve.

Now the hand is massaging my crotch.

It is working open the zip of my jeans.

The zip sounds incredibly loud, even with the engine noise.

I look at the driver and his eyes catch mine in the rear-view mirror. I can't. Not now, not with him there. But the hand is curling around my dick. Her hair is falling into my lap.

I check the mirror again. The driver winks at me.

Very gently, I ease her up.

'What? Whatsa matter?'

She sounds slurred and dreamy.

'Nothing. Shh. We're almost there.'

(This is a lie. We won't be there for a few minutes yet.)

I close my eyes and hug her. If I look again, he'll be there in the mirror, winking.

'Anywhere here's fine,' I say, trying to zip myself up without him seeing.

He pulls up to the kerb and I hand him a tenner, telling him to keep the change, and bustle us out of the cab.

The air is sharp. Suddenly I'm completely sober.

'Which one's yours?' she asks, twirling on the pavement and looking up at the houses.

A cat runs out from underneath a parked car.

I drape my jacket over her shoulders.

'It's a walk from here,' I say. 'Fancied a bit of fresh air.'

'Tell me a story,' she says.

So I start to tell her about me and what I used to do; my ex-job, my parents, my panic attacks and how something shifted inside me . . .

But she's no longer listening. She's stopped to pick up an empty crisp packet and post it through a letterbox.

Once we're through my door, I give her the choice of tea or coffee or vodka. She chooses black coffee with vodka in. Maybe it's just her drunkenness, but she seems more at home in my house than I am. The place is a mess of papers, clothes, plates and cans. I wasn't planning on bringing anyone home tonight. This sort of thing doesn't happen to me. My sheets are unwashed. I have no condoms. The bathroom is filthy. But she doesn't seem to mind. She's putting on music – Serge Gainsbourg's *Histoire de Melody Nelson*, the last thing I listened to – and slinking around in the mess. She picks books off the floor to read the spines. She knocks nothing over.

'You're a . . . What are you again?' she calls through.

I'm a bit scared of her.

In the kitchen, as the kettle comes to the boil, I take a big swig from the vodka bottle. I'm too sober and all I can think about is that winking taxi driver in the mirror. If I turn round, he'll be there in the doorway, gawping at me.

The vodka stings my ulcer.

'I work from home,' I say. 'It's pretty dull. You don't want to know.'

This is how we met. I was sat at a table in the club, not even able to peel the label off my £1 alcopop. I wasn't dancing. I didn't know why I'd come. And then a girl appeared. She'd been stood up, she said. I realise now how contrived that sounds. I guess it was. She contrived it. She approached me, asked if I was alone and sat down. (Maybe she was lying. But at the time, both of us piss-drunk, it seemed pretty plausible.) And I was left thinking, She has decided to like me, now I must decide to like her, too.

So I sat there, squinting at her, trying hard to like her.

It wasn't hard.

She's very pretty.

She has black hair cut just above the shoulder and black eyes and pitch white skin.

She has crooked teeth and thin piano-y fingers.

She dresses well.

She's confident.

She's smart.

(I have no idea what she's doing in my house.)

We get up from the table and go to a corner of the club. She puts her arms around my neck and sucks the collar of my shirt. A man comes over and taps her on the shoulder. He's thick-shouldered and brooding, his face in shadow.

He goes away. She's ignored him. We don't dance. We just stay there in the corner until the lights come on. Out in the street she stands at the kerb with her arm sticking into the road, one corner of her skirt hitched up. She's grinning at me. A taxi pulls over and I get into it, not knowing who she is, and then at some point I sober up.

Now I'm standing in the kitchen of my house waiting for the kettle to boil and there's a strange girl in my living room.

'What do you do again?' I call back.

This one I know. I remember it from earlier.

Everything is silent. Even the clock, ticking, is not making a noise.

'I'm in eyes,' she whispers.

She's snuck up behind me.

'I work in an optician's. It's rubbish. I should quit.'

I turn round. She's taken off her clothes.

Her eyes are wide and black. We aren't using a condom. I didn't ask if she's on the pill. She isn't blinking. She bites her lip. She's so loud she has to, to stop the sound of her from escaping out of her mouth and going through the walls and into the ears of next door's baby. Her eyes don't close. Instead they widen. They widen and widen again and just keep widening, until I am painfully sober and painfully aware of her watching me, and that once this is over, even if I never see her again, she will be able to remember the face of me fucking her. Here she is, scratching my back and biting her lip and no sound is coming from her mouth except breathing and her eyes do not close but instead they widen and widen and widen, until impossible, until they are like huge black lenses recording me.

Afterwards it's warm and quiet. Blue, 5 a.m. light. We lie on top of the sheets with our legs tangled and I wonder what we'll say when we wake up in the morning, hungover, not-drunk. Will we pretend it didn't happen?

(Maybe I ask the question out loud.)

'I won't regret this,' she says.

She's almost asleep.

'But sometimes I just need to do something and not think of the consequences.'

I'll lock the door, I think.

(The door doesn't have a lock.)

Somehow I'll trap us here.

'Hold on,' she says, suddenly awake and sitting up.

This is it, I think. She's leaving. She's left. She's gone into the street, naked. She's disappeared.

She leans across me, her head and arms doing something confusing over the side of the bed. I can hear the rattle and jingle of things in her handbag. She comes up holding a little plastic container, tilts her head forward and puts a finger to her eye, the left one, wiping it across the pupil.

'See,' she says, sticking the finger under my nose. 'I almost forgot.'

On the tip of her finger is a contact lens.

'I don't need these,' she says. 'I stole them from work. I just like putting things in my eyes.'

This is the first time I've noticed the scar. It starts at the curve of her shoulder and curls down around her arm. It is a darker nastier blue than the rest of her 3.15 a.m. skin. It's about six inches long.

She's asleep.

I lean over her, close enough for my breath to shuffle the wispy little hairs on her skin. There are more scars, too; lighter ones that criss-cross down her arm. But this one is the biggest.

I imagine a razor blade, a blot of blood on toilet paper and a locked bathroom door. I imagine other invisible scars that run underneath her skin. They shoot and crackle like a scar firework display.

She moves sometimes when she sleeps. She hunches and starts, as if someone in her dream is poking her with a stick or catching her in a net. She makes noises, she moans, but so far she hasn't woken up. Once she said something that sounded like 'Darren'. This is the fourth time she's slept in my bed. I really don't think she's going home now and I still don't know where her home is. She has a toothbrush here, a big bag of clothes and today a couple more boxes.

I lick the scar. It tastes of salt and shower gel.

There is a glass girl in my bed. If I ask too many questions she will shatter. So I'll wait for her to answer her own questions and in the meantime play join-the-freckles in the dark. Here are some of the freckles I have joined by myself, by not going to sleep:

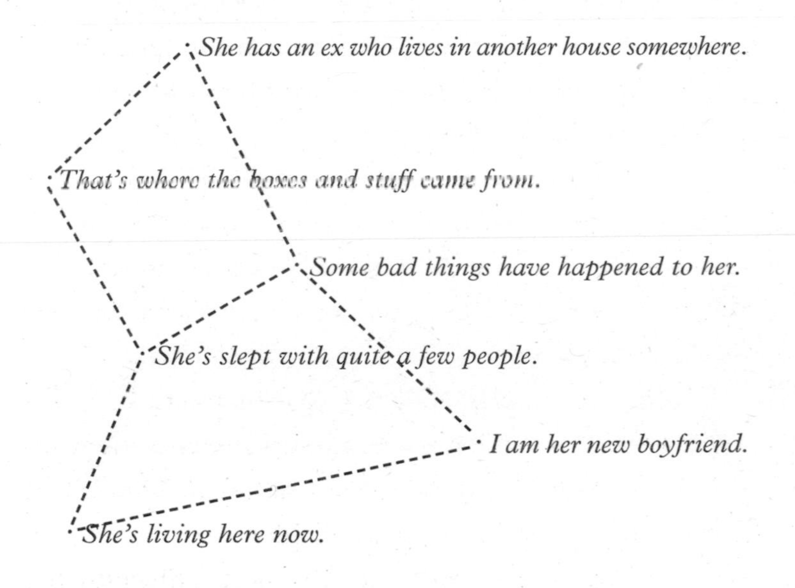

We went to the pub earlier – The Princess and Noose, my local – after she finished work. She asked what was wrong.

'Nothing,' I said.

'You know, you can ask me anything you want,' she said.

(I don't believe her.)

'Ask me a question,' she said.

So I asked, 'Would you like another drink?'

She smiled and said, 'Vodka and Coke.'

Stood elbow-to-elbow with all the shifty old men at the bar, I had to stop myself from turning round and checking she was still at the table.

Stop it, I told myself. Your luck has turned. Your luck has turned around on itself like an owl's head. She is not going to run away from you, at least not this evening.

Barry, one of the regulars, kept nudging me on the arm and asking who she was.

'She's my girlfriend,' I told him.

'About time, lad,' he said. 'We all had you pegged as a poof.'

Across the table, she kept on smiling at me.

(She looked very sad when she did it.)

Each time I went for a piss, I expected to get back to that table and find she'd gone. There wouldn't even be her drink there any more, and it would turn out to be some elaborate practical joke which everyone in the Noose is in on.

'Fuck's sake. What's wrong?' she says, suddenly, slamming her glass on the table for effect. Her lips curl at the edges. 'Something's up. Tell me.'

But I don't quite know how. I'm sitting on my hands, not even permitting myself a sip of my drink. If I do or say the wrong thing she will become a terrible accident. There are hard wooden floors in this pub. She'll shatter like a tower of toppled pint glasses, and everyone will cheer and look over, and even the fruit machines will stop rattling and blinking for a second.

'Come on,' she says, trying to get my hand out from under my arse by tugging at my jumper. 'Don't be such a coward.'

And before I can stop myself, I've said it. I've told her that I'm scared to touch her in case I do it wrong and she doesn't like it, and I've told her that I'm scared she will all of a sudden tell me to fuck off. I've told her how I feel like I need written permission before I can become comfortable enough with a person to know they won't mind me.

Her smile doesn't go away.

Her eyes don't stop looking sad when she smiles.

She doesn't say anything either, but she reaches for her bag and searches around in it and takes out a till receipt. She asks if I have a pen, which I don't. So she gets up and goes to the bar and comes back with a biro. She turns the till receipt over and writes something on the blank side. She chews her lip a bit as she writes.

She hands the receipt to me. In curly black biro it reads:

To whomever it may concern,
I hereby give the bearer of this note written permission to do whatever the hell he likes to me and I promise I won't mind. In fact, I'll probably like it quite a lot.
Very Sincerely,
Alice Holborn

After I read the note I stop sitting on my hands and take a big swig of my pint.

'You can't have always been like that,' she says, squeezing my fingers.

'I wasn't,' I lie.

'So what happened?'

I can't tell her the truth – that I've never really had a girlfriend before; that every person I've got involved with, I've scared away through jealousy and paranoia and the fear that I'll screw things up. I'm determined to make this work. I will reconstruct myself as a steady, stable and rational human being. I will be whatever she wants me to be. Alice, I'm yours if you want me.

'I don't know,' I say.

'Sometimes, if you want to do something, you should just do it,' she says, letting the lights above our table settle and glint in her eyes.

She sighs. She shuffles slightly. The receipt is in my wallet and my wallet is in the back pocket of my jeans and my jeans are hanging over the chair next to the bed. I move my hand from her hip and put it between her legs from behind. I push my middle finger slowly inside her.

She doesn't wake up.

She doesn't mind.

In fact, she probably likes it quite a lot.

We are laughing at the neighbours.

'Does this happen every night?' Alice says.

'Most nights,' I say. 'You'll get used to it.'

The woman neighbour is making a squealing sound.

The man neighbour is making a grunting sound.

'Help me,' the woman neighbour is saying. 'Help me. Help me.'

'How can I help you?' the man neighbour is saying.

Then more squealing, more grunting.

'It sounds like they're arguing and having sex at the same time,' I say. 'A sex argument.'

This makes Alice laugh. She curls up against me, puts her mouth on my chest and bites softly. I tickle her under the arms and she squeals. She blows a raspberry on my stomach.

'We should have a sex argument sometime,' she says.

'Okay,' I say. 'Help me.'

'How can I help you?' she says.

I make a squealing sound and she puts her hand over my mouth.

'Shh,' she says, 'they'll hear you.'

Then she makes a loud grunting sound.

'When I was little,' she says, 'when my parents were still in the country, there was this couple next door who argued all the time.'

She's never spoken about her parents before. Or her childhood.

'But that was horrible. It sounded like the man was killing the woman every night. Like he was bouncing her head off the walls. I'd lie in bed and wait for the sound of police cars.'

'Where are your parents now?' I say.

As soon as I've said it, it feels like the wrong thing to say. Something changes in her. Something freezes. Something snaps off. She shuffles in the bed, so we aren't touching as much any more. She turns to face the wall. I want to tell her that she doesn't have to answer if she doesn't want to. That she doesn't have to tell me anything at all.

'Not in England,' she says, and I leave it at that.

She was on the phone again. She takes her mobile into the bathroom and locks the door. She talks to somebody in a low whisper.

After she finishes work she comes back with boxes. Slowly the house is filling with her things. In the daytime I go through it all; books, clothes, hair products, CDs. No letters, diaries or photos.

It's not much to go on. I now know she likes Joy Division, Tom Waits and Erasure. I know she reads Albert Camus, Jane Austen and Anaïs Nin. I know she shops at Topshop, H&M and Dorothy Perkins.

I know nothing about her.

I sit there in my room – 'our room' – with her boxes around me, trying to find some sort of connection or piece of her in all this stuff. There are perfumes and three new kinds of soap in the bathroom. (What do her parents do?) There's a purple scrubbing-thing hanging from the shower. (Am I imagining it or does she somehow manage to steer any conversation away from 'her past'?) Her underwear comes mostly from Marks & Spencer. (Why did she suddenly start crying, that time last night when we were in bed?) She has about one hundred pairs of tights.

It's coming from her ex's place. It must be.

Darren.

He's bigger than me. He has short dark hair and wears a rugby shirt with his name written on the back. DARREN. The number 69. He is bullish and surly, his face perpetually in shadow.

(He is the man from the club that first night.)

Alice is still in love with him. She goes round to his house after work. Darren lives in a two-bed terrace, a kid's bike rusting in the grass out front. She rings the bell. The door opens. She goes inside.

'What do you want, then?' he says in the hall, his bottom lip flopping heavily as he speaks.

Darren reads *FHM*, cover to cover.

'I've come for the rest of my stuff,' she says, not making eye contact. She's afraid to. Instead she looks down at her shoes and then at his. Black boots next to chunky bright-white trainers.

Darren smells of aftershave. His skin is red and smooth and babyish. He backs against the wall, letting her pass.

Darren touches her arm.

Her skin remembers him.

Her skin sends something like a text message to her brain, which reads:

Fuck Darren 1 last time. Make sure u arent making a mistake.

Alice is in the bedroom now, putting things in a shoebox. Little things, all that's left; a bottle of perfume and a pen.

(Maybe she left them here on purpose.)

Darren stands in the doorway, watching.

His thoughts sound like gangsta rap, blunt and violent. His thoughts say things like *bitch* and *ass* in his head. They say *fuck that bitch's ass one last time*. There is an obvious beat behind his thoughts. It is Darren's heart.

'So this is really it, huh?' he says to her back.

Darren speaks like television; something American, with advert breaks and sponsorship.

Alice is leaning over the small mirrored dresser, catching his eye in the glass. She watches him walk around the bed, come up behind her and put his hands on her. He pushes her skirt up around her hips.

She doesn't stop him.

She just closes her eyes and breathes him in.

I am outside Darren's house, hiding behind a car. I've been here too long. It's getting cold. I can see nothing through the windows of Darren's house; they are icy black and unyielding.

I followed her out of work and onto the tram.

(When they come out, when they stand on the doorstep and have their tearful 'final goodbye' scene, I'll stand up and make my presence known. I'll go over to them, say something cutting and then somehow knock Darren's fucking teeth out.)

We rode the tram out of the city and into the winding redbrick residential area. Kids on bikes. Cornershops. King Size cigarettes. Bent old women. Shopping trolleys. I sat one carriage down, watching her through the little tram window.

(Once I've somehow knocked Darren's fucking teeth out, Alice will smile. She'll fall in love with me. Miraculously it will stop raining and someone in the distance will cheer. This will become the story we tell our grandchildren at Christmas, everyone laughing when they hear it and clinking their sherry glasses and clapping me on the back. 'Oh you!' they'll say encouragingly, finding me roguish but endearing.)

Then the door opens.

The door to Darren's house opens.

Alice steps onto the path.

A woman comes out, not Darren but a woman in a long ill-fitting jumper. The jumper has a bad likeness of Michael Bolton knitted into it. The woman has copper-red hair. It's Alice's mum, it has to be. They have the same black eyes, the same pale skin, the same slight crookedness to them. Their necks bend like flowers stood in bottles of vodka.

This is Alice's parents' house and Alice's mum is handing her a shoebox.

Why did she lie?

Her mum is standing in the doorway in a Michael Bolton jumper.

Her parents are not abroad.

I want to jump and wave and scream. I want her to know I've followed her here, that I don't trust her and I still think there's a bloke called Darren somewhere who she used to live with and who she's screwing on the side.

But instead I just stay crouched behind the car.

I feel awful enough to buy some cheap supermarket flowers on the way back home.

In time she'll tell me everything; about her mum, her ex-boyfriends, her life before me. She will open up slowly, like time-lapse photography. She will begin to feel safe and comfortable and start telling the truth. She will start to need me.

But for this to happen, I must give her space.

I must be quiet and calm; not jealous or possessive or judging.

Most of all, I mustn't scare her away.

(I know it's not been long but I don't know what I'd do if she left.)

When Alice comes she pulls me tight against her, so I can feel the trembling of her body, her arms and legs wrapped around me, her hair in my face, her chin digging hard into my shoulder. This is what turns me on the most. It makes me come too. I'm not like Will, probably turned on by some kind of out-of-body sex image; a graphic full-on porno vision of himself 'slamming it into some girl'. What I want isn't visual. What I want is cloudy and indistinct. It exists somewhere at the centre of her. It is the part of her that wants me too.

She stays lying on top of me afterwards, with her head resting against my head.

I feel safe, buried underneath her. If we could somehow just continue to stay like this – if we could find a way to never have to eat or drink or leave the room, and if this was a goal we could realistically work towards and achieve, like we could somehow write off and apply for it, a kind of 'sex bursary' or something – I think I'd be happy.

We don't talk for a long time.

It's Sunday. Early afternoon.

'I'm going to ask you something,' she says.

'Okay,' I say.

'And I want you to think about it really hard and then answer truthfully.'

'Okay,' I say.

A pause.

'Do you love me?' she says.

Christ.

We've only been together two weeks.

We've not used the word before. I'd be scared to, but it sounds, when she says it, not strange or cheap or like something off the television. Maybe it's because she doesn't have to speak very loudly and her head is so close to mine and about 90 per cent of her speech is just soft warm breath in my car.

'Yeah,' I say.

I want to say the word 'love', too. I want to really, really badly, but I can't.

'How about you?' I say, instead.

I feel the muscles clench in her back.

I feel something change inside her.

I wait for her to answer.

'I don't know,' she says, finally.

Everything seems suddenly not-moving and very far away.

'Okay,' I say.

My voice has gone quiet and strange-sounding, like I'm speaking long-distance.

'God,' she says, 'I'm joking.'

But she feels about four hundred miles away from me.

I can't see her face. I can't see if she's smiling when she says this.

'Bloody hell. Of course I do.'

She lifts her head up and looks me in the eyes. Her eyes are so clear and large and black, it feels as if my whole face could disappear into them. She props herself up on her elbow and brushes my hair with her hand.

'Come here,' she says and kisses me. 'It was a crap joke. I think I saw it in some film or something. Christ. Lighten up.'

Now she only feels about four hundred metres away from me, like we're standing at opposite ends of an empty field and waving at each other.

She starts to walk across the field by kissing me and biting my neck.

'I'm sorry,' she whispers occasionally on the way. 'I'm sorry.'

‘They’re big,’ she says with the toothbrush in her mouth. ‘They don’t go hard.’

Then she spits, runs the tap.

My fingers are pinching her nipples. Her eyes look into mine in the mirror. We’re going to bed next. We’ve washed our faces and in the morning she’ll have to get up and go to work, and I will hang around all day in the house, missing her and looking at the clock.

The cold tap rattles. I put my fingers under the water and touch some more against her nipple; against the oval chocolate-red aureole and large puckered teat. She shivers but doesn’t pull away.

‘Told you,’ she says, a fleck of toothpaste foam on her lower lip. ‘I’m not that pretty. Sometimes I don’t even know why you like me.’

I don't reply. I'm not here. I'm watching this on TV.

I'm watching my fingers touch the drips of water to her skin in the mirror.

This is someone else's hand, I think, not mine. This hand is acting out the mirror of my actions and her nipple is doing the opposite of hardening.

How in love we were.

One night in bed she tells me how an ex-boyfriend talked her into doing porn. He had this mate who worked for a website. It would all be completely anonymous.

'It was a few years ago.'

She's whispering.

It's so dark I can hardly see her face, so quiet I can hear empty crisp packets wisping along the street outside our house. Two in the morning. Her breath smells acidic. My hand is on her hip.

'I hardly knew him, really. We were only together for a couple of months.'

I want to know and I don't want to know.

'What did you do?' I ask.

'Just sex,' she says. 'His mate lent him a camera and one night he filmed me, you know . . . as he fucked me.

It was for this amateurs' site. All he had to do was make sure he held the camera steady. It wasn't art. I didn't talk.'

I want to know the specifics. I want to know if she went down on him first. I want to know what positions they used. I want to know if he came inside her or if, like in most porn I'd seen, he came on her face or her tits. But I can't ask. Her voice is small and shaky. My hand moves from her hip.

'Did you watch the tape afterwards?'

'No. He did. He asked me if I wanted to see it and I said no. So he gave it to his mate and it got used, apparently.'

How about her? Did *she* get used? Did she get paid?

(Where is my hand going?)

More than anything, I want to ask what the site's called. Is the film still there? Is someone watching it as we speak?

'Why did you do it?'

My heart is hammering. I can see stills, freeze-frames, flashes of her in graphic sexual positions. I can see her body splintered into a lurid sequence of thumbnail photographs. The images burn. They do not go away. I'm disgusted and aroused.

(My hand's between her legs.)

She doesn't answer. Instead, she kisses me and I taste the acid on her tongue. We don't mention it again.

She chooses the time and place for these admissions, not me.

She chooses how much or how little she tells me.

This is not her first whispered, two-in-the-morning confession.

In the morning I lie in bed and listen to the sound of her getting ready for work. Just before she leaves, she comes back into the room, leans over the bed and kisses me on the forehead.

'I think you're prime rib,' she whispers in my ear.

Then she's gone.

I get out of bed and put on my dressing gown. I go into the second bedroom, the empty one. I redraw the curtains and sit down at the computer and log onto the internet.

The clip is out there, somewhere.

A thousand grubby old men are clicking on it right now.

It's just a process of elimination.

I will find that clip if it kills me.

I will not give up.

It will be my new job.

I will find the clip.

I want to watch it. I want to see Alice's face. I want to see if she looks different with someone else, if she enjoys it more. I want to see her without her seeing me. Then I'll destroy it; somehow I'll remove her from the internet. She should just be with me now, not me and anyone else who accidentally clicks on her.

So I begin to Google my way through hundreds of amateur porn sites.

Babes movies – real amateur babes!
young british amateur first timer girls – webcams – videos – this is the real deal! These girls are young and . . .
www.britamateursexmovie.com – 33k – Cached – Similar pages – Note this

Hot British Fuck Movies
Free Preview Pictures and Movies of British couples in amateur sex situations. Couple on bench – Couple in the woods – Couple . . .
www.uksexsituations.com/preview.html – 18k – Cached – Similar pages – Note this

Hardcore Amateur SEX!
I filmed my ex! 100% real amateur footage, submitted by bitter ex-boyfriends! These girls are horny and wild! No credit card needed . . .
www.ex-sex-frenzy.com/Alice.html – 44k – Cached – Similar pages – Note this

Red Hot Action With British Amateur Babes
These young beauties will do anything . . . Helen, 16 pics, 5 vids (mpg) –
Chloe, 22pics, 2 vids (mpg) – Alice, 0 pics, 1 vid . . .
www.babes-amateurs-xxx.com – 21k – Cached – Similar pages – Note this

I go through page after page, finding nothing, as a thousand other men around the world stumble unwittingly across her image. They hover their cursors over her thumbnail and double-click. They download her. Sat in dark musty rooms, they squirm in their seats as she pants and pouts for the camera.

Alice stares out of the screen; not at them, not at anything. Her eyes are wide and black and blank.

She throws back her head and yelps with pleasure.

I meet her after work at this vodka bar just off Market Square. Walking into town, I feel as delicate and raw as new skin after a plaster is removed. I can still see images from websites, hundreds of girls staring out blindly from my computer screen.

My head is filled to bursting with other people's amateur ex-girlfriends.

She's slouched on a sofa next to another girl. They spot me and Alice gives a loose-wristed wave. They're both drunk off the 6 o'clock cocktail happy hour.

It's just gone seven, so I buy a pint and swig it quickly, trying to catch up.

I'm introduced. William, this is Lauren. Lauren also works at the optician's. Lauren thinks working at the optician's is rubbish, too. Lauren wonders what *you* do for a living.

'I work from home,' I tell her.

'Oh yeah?' Lauren says, raising her eyebrow. 'What do you do?'

'It's really dull,' I say. 'You wouldn't want to know.'

'Try me,' Lauren says.

So I say that I do something with 'systems' – trying to drop in vague technical words like 'protocol' and 'analysis' and 'statistics'.

Lauren furrows her brow. Something doesn't sound quite right about this. Something doesn't add up, and Lauren can't put her finger on it.

'How was your day?' I ask Alice, trying to change the subject, putting my hand on her knee and rubbing it, feeling the static-y friction of my thumb against her tights, trying to act normal but feeling way too conscious that everything I'm doing is an act.

Lauren's still looking.

Lauren will not stop looking at me.

Lauren thinks I'm a liar, a dirty perv.

It's written all over my face. It's obvious what I did all day.

And Lauren will tell Alice this the next time they're alone – the next time they go off to the toilets, maybe – she'll tell Alice what I really did with my afternoon and Alice will freak out and leave me.

At eight the bar starts filling up. Big blokes in Ted Baker shirts. Shaved heads. Ibiza tans.

Alice kisses me, forcing her tongue into my mouth. She tastes of Seabreeze. Her teeth are as cold as crushed ice.

I open my eyes for a second and Lauren's staring at us. She looks uncomfortable.

Once we've finished, Lauren makes a show of looking at the clock, at her mobile and suddenly remembering something.

'Oh god,' she says, 'I'd better shoot . . .' standing up with half her cocktail still on the table.

'Alright,' Alice says, smiling. 'See you tomorrow.'

Before Lauren's even out the door, Alice has taken my hand and put it under her top. She's not wearing a bra. She buries her head in the crook of my neck and mumbles something.

She gets like this, usually once she's had a few. She gets turned on, I think, by the idea of people watching.

I accidentally gaze into the black piss-hole eyes of a bloke at the bar.

He doesn't blink.

I look away, but I can still feel him there, staring at me.

It feels like everyone in the bar – everyone in the world – is looking.

I feel sick and cold.

She's almost sitting on my lap.

She's winding herself around me, kissing my neck and tonguing my Adam's apple.

‘Get a room!’ the bloke at the bar shouts and a few people cheer in agreement.

So, after one last vodka shot, we do. We take a taxi home and I have to help her out of it. She slings her arm across my shoulder and leans in heavily.

I walk her to the bathroom.

She locks herself in.

‘You alright?’ I call through the door after a while.

Inside I can hear crying.

I switch on the telly.

I turn it up.

She comes out and sits next to me on the sofa. I turn down the telly. She leans her head against my shoulder, smelling of soap, her eyes red and raw. I put my arm around her. We watch a news story about Third World debt. My hand is near her boob. She sniffs. I reach down and cup it in my palm, feeling its sad quiet weight.

‘Don’t,’ she says, so I drop it.

It isn't her, but it's close. She smiles at you. Her teeth are neat. They are bleached a high-contrast white. She shakes the hair out of her eyes. She is moving slowly, sliding a bra strap delicately off her shoulder. Her eyes are wide and black. She isn't nervous. There is no sound except your breathing. Off slides the other strap. This isn't her. It isn't. But it's the closest yet. She licks her lips and laughs to herself. Then she reaches behind her back, unclasps the bra and holds it to her breasts. She pouts like a Marilyn Monroe photocopy. She moves closer, smiles again and lets the . . .

She freezes. Frantically, you click on the next file. You're fumbling because the mouse is in your left hand. Four in the afternoon. The curtains are drawn. The room smells warm and musty. A toilet roll stands next to the computer.

. . . bra fall to the floor. You lean up close to the screen and squint. Her nipples are too small. They're a pinky-red colour. She takes them in her fingertips and pinches. She giggles silently. The camera moves down her belly. Her fingers follow it towards her knickers. She hooks her thumbs under the strip of flimsy black elastic and wiggles, rubbing her thighs together. You can see fine down on her skin. There is no chicken-leg birthmark on her thigh, though, and no mole next to her belly button. She bends forward as she slides off the knickers, the top of her head obscuring . . .

Again, she stops. You grope for a wad of toilet paper with your non-mouse hand. Was that the letterbox in the hall? Quickly, you check the curtains for gaps. It's just the free paper, the paperboy walking back down the path. Alice won't be home for another hour yet. So you click on clip three (which is all Virgin British Beavers will give you without a credit card).

. . . the view. She steps out of her knickers and sits back on the bed. The camera moves between her thighs. You inch your nose up against the screen. Her pubic hair is black. It's clipped. Her lips are shaved. She prises them apart with shiny lacquer-pink nails and sinks in a middle finger. The screen is warm. It buzzes against the tip of your nose and up this close she pixellates and distorts. She begins to look like a game of Tetris. So you pull your head away again, just enough, but wish you could force it past the plastic and into the volcanic red of her cunt.

Alice, Alice, Alice, you think, as your eyes close, and the curtains and the free paper and the headache are swallowed in a warm, swelling, consuming nothing.

I button my jeans and stand. My spine crackles. I open the curtains and have a look into the street. An old bloke stands at the end of our path, waiting for his dog to finish crapping on the pavement.

In the bathroom, I try to piss without catching the reflection of my red-raw, semi-erect dick in the mirror. This is impossible. The mirror faces you. It confronts you. It is a gaping glass eye, streaked with stray toothpaste spittle and the wet flicks of her hair from drying. It sits just next to the toilet, reflecting me. Pissing should be enough, surely? Pissing and shitting and being an animal should be enough without having to watch yourself as you do it. The mirror was there when I moved in. It has something to do with feng shui, Alice reckons.

My dick looks how I imagine a bloated drowned body might look.

I take down the mirror and carry it into the yard. I lean it against the wall, the one where the child of a previous tenant drew a Ninja Turtle in chalk. I stand back to admire my work. That's more like it. Let nature have its stupid cock reflected back at it. See how the leaves and slugs and bottle tops like it for a change.

I do nothing the rest of the day.

I watch TV.

I eat Rich Tea biscuits.

I am repeatedly haunted by the image of a blonde girl fucking herself with a shoe.

At a quarter to six Alice gets home from work.

'Good day?' I call over my shoulder.

She doesn't answer. She takes off her coat, steps out of her boots and goes into the bathroom.

After a pause, the toilet flushes.

'Where's the mirror gone?' she says.

'It's in the yard,' I say. 'I put it there.'

I wait for her to ask why.

I almost *want* her to ask why.

(I don't know what I'll say if she does.)

But she just puts on her boots, goes into the yard and carries it back to the bathroom.

In bed we listen to one of Alice's CDs. Some sort of electronica. She's leafing through a fashion magazine which is about 80 per cent adverts. I'm watching the pages turn from the corner of my eye.

'Hold on,' I say, laying my palm flat across the magazine.

'What?' she says.

I lean over, pretending to take a closer look at a redheaded model in a photo shoot.

'What?' she says. 'What is it?'

'Nothing,' I say, letting go of the magazine. 'Just looked a bit like someone I knew.'

I wait.

The silence swells around us.

'Like who?' she says eventually.

'Oh, just some girl I used to go out with.'

'Right,' says Alice and turns the page. She starts to read an article on celebrity collagen injections.

Is that it? 'Right', as if she didn't believe me? Why shouldn't I have an ex somewhere who looks a bit like the girl in her magazine?

I had a whole relationship planned, ready to tell her; a girl I met at an old job – Carol – who ended up moving to London. We lived together for almost a year and then things finished amicably. It was her job, not me, that made her unhappy and caused the move. We tried things long-distance for a bit, but it didn't work out. We're still friends but have kind of lost touch.

'Carol,' I say, out loud.

'What?' she says, looking up from the article.

'Carol. That was the girl's name. The one I went out with.'

'Great,' she says.

I leave a dramatic pause.

'We used to live together for a bit.'

'Fantastic.'

'And then she had to move to London.'

'Wonderful.'

'I'm still in touch with her.' Alice has closed the magazine. 'But not like that. Just as friends.'

She flips off the covers and gets out of bed.

She walks out of the room. I think she's going to the toilet, but then I hear the sound of her walking down the stairs and across the hall and into the kitchen. I wait for a running tap or the clink of a plate on the countertop.

Nothing.

I wait a long time.

Still nothing.

Alice is down there in the kitchen, probably sat at the table with her head in her hands, hating Carol, seeing images of me and her in bed together, at the park, laughing, kissing, sharing an ice-cream . . .

Carol, fucking Carol, Alice is thinking, biting her lip and wringing her hands and wanting to smash Carol's knees and stick hot pins in her eyes.

I am something worth getting jealous over, I think.

I've won.

Alice is definitely in love with me.

Will calls round unexpectedly. Three in the afternoon. Alice is at work. I'm upstairs in the empty second bedroom, using the computer. The screen is full of pop-up windows. [Teen Sex Fiesta] [Housewife Pool Party] When I try to close them, more appear in their place. I'm peering down from a crack in the curtains. Will rings the doorbell a second time. I wait for him to go away. But Will is persistent. He steps back. He looks up at the window. He spots me and waves.

I turn off the monitor and walk down the stairs, feeling shifty and sore-eyed.

'Just wanted to see how your new life was going,' he says when I open the door.

I lead him through to the living room.

He sits down on the sofa and starts rolling a fag.

'Well?' he says.

'Fine,' I say. 'It's going fine.' [Abigail's Fuck Playground] 'Drink?'

'Can't stop,' he says. 'Meeting some bloke in town in a minute. Might have another exhibition lined up.'

'How's Katrina?' I say. [Hardcore Ass Fest]

'Who?' he says.

'The girl you introduced me to the other week.'

'Oh, Kat*ri*na,' he says, pronouncing it differently. 'Don't ask.'

So I don't.

Will lights his roll-up and looks around for an ashtray. He spots something of Alice's, a CD on the coffee table.

'Since when did you start liking Erasure?' he says.

'They're alright,' I lie.

He picks up a half-empty mug of tea and taps his ash into it. He puts it down by his foot.

'It smells different in here,' he says, raising an eyebrow and looking around the room.

'How do you mean?'

'And it's tidier, too.'

Then he notices a pair of Alice's trainers under the coffee table.

'Bloody hell,' he says. 'Are you *seeing* someone?'

'Why do you make it sound so unbelievable?' I say. [Horny Midwives, Now Online!]

'Because in the however-many years I've known you, you've *never* seen anyone.'

'Well, now I am.'

'Bloody hell,' he says again, smiling and shaking his head.

He drops his fag end into the mug.

'You'll have to introduce us sometime,' he says, standing.

I walk him out to the [One Hundred Free Snatch Movies] door.

'Will,' I say. 'If you *do* ever meet her, don't mention that I'm unemployed, okay? I kind of told her I work from home.'

'Yeah, yeah, whatever,' he says, not really listening. 'Before I forget . . . The other reason I came round . . . Is there any chance you could water my plants one day next week? I'm off to Paris for a bit, you see. Some exhibition thing. The old bint from next door was lined up to do it, but she died last night.'

He hands me a key.

'Cheers, mate,' he says and walks off down the path.

The phone is ringing in the hall. The phone hardly ever rings now. I'm in the living room, watching telly. Alice is in the kitchen. It's her turn to cook.

The phone is nearer to the kitchen than it is to the living room.

It might just be cold-calling, but it might be someone from my old job.

It might be my boss.

I pick up on the third ring.

'Hello, William.'

It's my parents.

'We've put you on speakerphone.'

'Hi,' I say, speaking as quietly as I can, pressing the receiver against my mouth.

Alice comes to the doorway, holding a wooden

spoon. She watches me for a second, then goes back into the kitchen.

'How's things?' says my mum.

'Alright.'

'How's work?' says my dad.

'Not bad.'

I've not told them about leaving my job or about Alice.

If I tell them about the job, I'll become a disappointment; immature and irresponsible, a child still.

If I tell them about Alice, they'll ask about her every time they call. They'll want to meet her. And if Alice leaves – if I scare her away somehow – it will be like all the other girls I've mentioned to them; the ones I *did* scare off, the ones I had to pretend I was still seeing for months afterwards.

So I answer their questions in monosyllables, telling them pretty much nothing, just that I'm tired, that work is 'quite demanding' at the moment and that I really have very little to report. I keep my voice low, hoping it doesn't carry through to the kitchen.

When I hang up, Alice reappears in the doorway.

'Who was that?' she says.

'My friend, Will,' I say.

'Two Wills, eh?' she says. 'I thought you didn't have any friends.'

We had a not-exactly-argument the other night, about how we never go out or do anything or meet anyone new. I told her that the way my job worked, I hardly met anyone at all. I told her I'd lost touch with all my old friends. I said I was quite happy to do something with *her* friends if she wanted; have them over to dinner, maybe. She said all the people at the optician's were twats.

'He's been out of the country for a while,' I say.

'What does he do?'

'He's an artist.'

Will's still out of the country. He gets back later this week. (I've not watered his plants yet.) I imagine them meeting. Will laying on the charm. Alice disliking him. The bus ride home afterwards. 'That friend of yours was a bit of a smarmy prick, wasn't he?' I'll introduce them.

By meeting Will, I think, Alice might love me even more.

Will's house smells of roll-ups and aftershave. I water his plants from a chipped tea-stained *Ghostbusters 2* mug. The only plants I can find downstairs are a wilting rubber plant in the living room and a tall spindly thing in the kitchen which looks dead already. It has fairy lights wrapped around its branches. I pour extra water into the pot, imagining Will getting electrocuted the next time he turns it on.

Bird paintings are hanging in the living room.

In the hall, a series of female nudes.

I look closely at the face of one of them, at the crude black lines of her cheeks and neck, the rough swirls and dots of her eyes. Even reduced to a few brush-strokes, she looks familiar; most likely one of the hundred girls Will's introduced me to in the past. I guess I still find it hard to take him seriously as an artist – I can remember us getting pissed on cheap cider in the car park behind his house, sixteen years old. Back then, Will wanted to be a singer. He wanted to be Nick Cave. He had this ridiculous messed-up haircut, and he used to talk incessantly about how, if he started a band, he'd be 'swimming in pussy'. Then he did alright at college, went off to Glasgow and came back an artist.

I go upstairs. I've never been upstairs in this house before.

No plants in the bedroom. Just a bed, a dresser, a full-length mirror and clothes all over the floor. A tiger-print bedspread. On the bedside table, a full ashtray, an empty bottle of wine and a dog-eared copy of *Mr Nice* by Howard Marks.

No plants in the bathroom, either.

I go into the final room. Will's studio. Canvases and bits of wood rest against the walls. The floor is covered with a paint-flecked old sheet which is taped to the carpet. An empty easel stands in the middle of the room. By the window is a desk with a laptop and a cheap stereo on it.

I sit down.

I turn on Will's computer.

He has a photograph of Anna Karina as his desktop.

I go to 'My Computer'.

I double-click.

I open 'My Documents'.

I open 'My Pictures'.

I don't know what I'm expecting to find.

The window fills with folders. They're not named, just dated. I open the first one: '09/01/07'.

A photo of Will, stood in front of the full-length mirror in his bedroom. He holds a digital camera in one hand. His shirt is unbuttoned a bit, so you can see wisps of his scraggly chest hair. He looks into the lens, his head tilted and one eyebrow raised.

I click 'Next'.

Will, again, now with his shirt completely unbuttoned. His non-camera hand rests, posed, on his hip. His mouth is curled into a snarl, showing off his yellowed wonky teeth. It looks like he's swept his hair back with his hand between photos.

'Next'.

Will, with his top off, leaning back on the bed. His flies are unzipped, his belt unbuckled, black hair curling in a line over his beer gut. He's thrust his legs wide apart and he's stroking his chest with his free hand like he thinks he's in a Prince video or something. His chest looks like it's been oiled. I squint at the picture and make out a bottle of baby lotion lying on the tiger-print bedspread behind him. His mouth is open, his tongue flopping out 'seductively'.

Christ.

I turn off the computer and stand up, feeling like he could walk in at any moment.

On my way out, I leave a note on the kitchen table:

Will,

Plants watered. Give us a ring when you get back. Alice would really like to meet you.

Will

The bathroom is bare. A stark cold white. There is nothing in this bathroom – absolutely piss-all – that gives the impression a man uses it, ever, has even used it the once. There's no towel, for instance.

So how does he dry himself?

Helen imagines he must get out of the shower and just sort of stand there. Or he doesn't dry himself at all and just puts his clothes on still wet. This leads Helen to imagine his naked body. Slight and pale, she imagines. All ribs and goosebumps. A long thin cock with wiry black hair.

There is no mirror.

She pulls up her skirt and sits down. Her eyes drift around the room.

There is no toothbrush or toothpaste by the sink, just the remains of a moth, its wings stuck to the porcelain.

If his teeth had been bad, Helen would've noticed. So what does he clean them with, then? His finger?

There is no soap.

Helen can't remember him smelling bad or smelling of anything at all. She lifts her sleeve and sniffs it; lemons, clouds and fabric softener. This is a bad habit of hers. She's sniffed sleeves ever since first school.

Helen decides on a fag. She's going to need one if she's to get through another half an hour of that looking. She digs the packet out of her handbag and lights one, tapping the first speckles of ash into the sink. What about the story he wanted her to tell? Darren and the casino and the taxi. So far he's said hardly anything. The wisp and smell of the fag ghosts round the bathroom like a cat of smoke, rubbing itself against the pipes and tiles. It purrs its way down the back of her throat.

This sparseness, bareness, or whatever you want to call it, is not confined to the bathroom either. It hangs over the whole house (what Helen's seen of it). To get to the bathroom you have to walk along a very bare corridor and up a very bare staircase. The carpets are gone. There is nothing on the windowsills except layers of thick grey dust and a couple of dead flies. The only furniture is stained and battered and old-fashioned, like it's been rescued out of skips. There are empty cans and food containers everywhere, but they don't count.

She thinks she hears something; a soft foot on a floorboard. So she turns on the tap and runs her fag under it. With her other hand she shoos away the smoke cat. She wonders if William or Will or whoever he is is pressed up against the door, listening to the glassy tinkle of her piss.

She's been here now a good half an hour and he still hasn't said anything much. He's spent most of the time just looking at her.

First of all, after she came in, after she sat down in the armchair, he asked whether she'd like a cup of tea.

'Yes,' she'd said. 'A cup of tea would be nice.'

William disappeared into the kitchen.

And once he was gone, Helen noticed something. She noticed that there felt more of him when he was out of the room than when he was in it. As if – by leaving – he'd moved up the sofa towards her.

Helen rooted around in her handbag for her fags and lighter. There was no ashtray she could see and no smell of cigarettes in the house, but she was sure he wouldn't mind. The men didn't usually mind. She planned to tap the ash into her cupped palm, like something she'd seen in an old film. By the time the fag was stuck between her lips and the lit lighter inches away from it, William had finished making the tea. He was on his way back to the living room.

Helen lit the fag.

William opened the door.

She breathed in.

He stepped into the room.

She breathed out.

The feeling of him shuffled away one place down the sofa.

'Don't smoke,' he said.

He put a mug of tea on the wobbly tea-ringed old table in front of her and sat down. He sat down in the same place the feeling of him had moved to.

Helen let her cigarette burn for a few more seconds, looking around for something to stub her fag in. She would've liked one more drag but she didn't dare.

'Put it in this,' said William, holding out an old empty mug.

Helen ground out her fag. She took a sip of tea. It wasn't sweet enough. She needed it so sweet all you could taste was sugar. William didn't touch his.

Then they sat there for ages, not speaking. Helen drawing out her tea – slowly, slowly, slowly – and even once it was cold, lifting and sipping it, because once that was gone there'd be nothing. What about the story? What about Darren and the casino?

He'd watched her close enough to make her feel like she was in a science video of someone drinking a cup of tea. And now she is utterly convinced that he's listening to her piss from behind the bathroom door.

It's when Helen stands to flush that she sees it. A single black pube stuck to the inside rim of the toilet. It's not one of hers. It's long and black and crooked.

She bends down. It makes her feel better. The pube. The bit of him. It looks sad.

She smiles at it. The pube doesn't smile back. A milky droplet of water dangles from it, at one end.

Helen straightens up. She washes her hands (without soap), then dries them on her skirt. When she opens the door, she's ready to say 'Hi' or something if she finds him standing in the doorway.

Instead she finds nothing, just the empty hall.

Helen goes into Barnardo's. The man she hopes might one day be her husband isn't working. Two old ladies stand behind the counter, listening to the radio and pricing books in pencil.

She goes up and down the shelves of ornaments, looking for something. She will know what it is when she sees it. It is not a teapot or a glass ballet-dancer figurine or a set of Yorkshire Dales placemats. Helen looks carefully at the objects, making sure the thing she's looking for is not hidden behind some other thing or inside it.

Corrine should be home now. Tonight is one of Corrine's two week nights off. Helen wants to go home and find Corrine sat on the sofa underneath a big orange duvet, and for Corrine to look at her when she comes in and say, 'Come 'ere,' and hold the duvet open for Helen to get under.

There'll be some film on – something corny like *Grease* or *The King and I* – and they'll make jokes about John Travolta's hips or Yul Brynner's head and hold hands under the duvet.

Corrine doesn't approve of what Helen does. She's never said this out loud; Helen's not even 100 per cent sure that she *knows* what Helen does. But, still, she gets the impression sometimes.

Corrine is hard and cold. Corrine is like a 70p porcelain biscuit jar.

When Helen answered the advert – Female housemate wanted, to share with quiet female, 26, smoker. Single room. £200ppw. Bills inclusive. – Corrine sat her down on the sofa and asked her a series of cold hard biscuit-jar questions.

What do you do?

(I'm an actress.)

And you get regular work?

(I have done so far.)

How clean and tidy are you?

Helen waited for a joke.

No joke came.

Despite all this, Corrine is Helen's best friend because – apart from Duncan and her mum – Corrine is the only person who doesn't call her Clair.

* * *

Corrine is home when Helen gets back. She's on the sofa, watching TV. No duvet, though. No corny film. Corrine has music television playing and she's reading a magazine and drinking a cup of tea.

'How was your day?' Corrine asks.

Helen sits down on the sofa. She looks at Corrine's bare blotchy legs and then at the TV. Corrine has a voice like a nail file, one which smoothes away anything rough or unnecessary.

Helen thinks about her day.

She thinks about Will or William and that bare house. How there wasn't even a smell she could find anywhere. She thinks about the pube stuck to the toilet. She thinks about sitting back down on the sofa and being asked to tell the story. She told it well, she thought. Her voice shook a bit, but that added to the effect. By the end of it, his eyes were closed and he might have been smiling.

He'd asked if she wore coloured contacts to make her eyes blue, and Helen flinched, feeling more exposed than if she'd been lying on her back with her legs over her shoulders and a camera pointing at her crotch.

Yes, she'd said, and he'd asked her to take them out. Good, he'd said, looking at her real eyes, her other eyes, at *Clair*'s eyes – dull black-brown pebbles.

'It was alright,' she tells Corrine, and Corrine nods and sips her tea.

'There's half a pizza left in the oven,' says Corrine.

'Thanks,' says Helen, feeling like she'll never be able to eat anything again for the rest of her life.

In her room, Helen stands in front of the Ethan Hawke picture. He looks sideways, avoids her. To catch his eye, she would need to go right into the corner of the room, by the window, and over there she wouldn't be able to see him any more.

'Look at me,' she says in her head. 'Look me in the eye, Ethan.'

This is a new scene in the film, a scene you never see, awkward and pointless. It doesn't 'move the plot along'. It lasts about five minutes – one single pointless take of nothing happening – and then Helen sits at her desk and turns on her computer. She checks her emails.

Nothing.

She checks the site where people from her old school post information about themselves.

It says Angela Lawrence is buying a house with her boyfriend. It doesn't say who Angela Lawrence's boyfriend is. Helen tries to remember Angela Lawrence. She opens the profile. 'No photos uploaded by this member'. The screen urges Helen to get in touch. It suggests some 'ice breakers'.

Angela Lawrence, Angela Lawrence. Helen finally remembers a girl in the front row of Maths, with lank black hair and a full-moon face, a salt-and-vinegar complexion. She logs out.

She logs in to the adult contacts site and checks her message box. There are two new replies to her profile:

> [Posted from Sexwand_52 @ 20:19] You are a slut. You like it up the ass. You are a horny ass tramp. Asssssssssssss sssssssssssssssssssssssssssssssssssssssssssssssss sssssssssssssssssssssssssssssssssssssssssssssssss sssssssssssssssssssssssss

and

> [Posted from WR @ 21:05] I am happy with our meeting today. If you come back next Tuesday, I will pay you £500 cash to have sex with you and film it. Do not wear your contact lenses. Get your hair cut to just above the shoulder and dye it black. I will only pay you if you do these things.

Helen clicks 'Reply'.

Helen books herself an appointment over the phone; four o'clock with Laura. She's decided to try a new place. Until then she's walking around town looking in windows and smoking fags and fingering mobiles in the Orange shop. It's Monday. If she goes back then she's going back tomorrow. She needs a haircut, anyway. She needs to keep herself smart. She would have got one whatever she was planning. In her hand she holds a Sainsbury's bag with a home hair-dye kit inside.

Boots have a better selection, but Helen hasn't been back into Boots since she left. If she did, Sandra Jones would be sitting at the till near the door. Sandra Jones would give her a look; she'd roll her eyes and pretend not to recognise her. She'd go *uh* with her mouth, then look away.

Superdrug have a better selection, too, but about half a year ago she went home with a man she met in a night-club who claimed he worked there as store security. Since then she hasn't even walked down the street that Superdrug's on, because store security always seem to stand around in the doorways.

Helen needs to get out of this city, to somewhere huge and anonymous. She wishes she could live in a rain-forest or the sky.

The clock in Market Square chimes the quarter hour.

At the salon, Helen gets sat down by the window and asked if she'd like tea or a coffee or anything ('Tea please, five sugars'). Laura will be over in a sec. She looks at her-self in the mirror, her washed hair hanging wet and rough.

What does she think of William or Will or whoever he is? He seemed sad. He seemed like her, like he was trapped in that house, because every time he went out there'd be someone who knew him, someone he didn't want to see.

Does she like him a bit? Can you like a pervert? That's what Helen calls them; the men with saggy trousers and stains on their jumpers who invite her in and make her do things. The Perverts. They're like awk-ward ostracised uncles that no one wants round for Christmas. They send you gift vouchers in nondescript cards and stay indoors with microwave meals.

When Laura comes to cut her hair – says 'Hello' and 'How would you like it, then?' and begins lifting up a bit of her hair – it takes Helen a moment to work it out. She feels like she's looking at herself or something. Then she realises.

It's Laura Castle.

The one from school.

The pasty Helen ate earlier becomes a snowball in her belly.

'Well?' Laura Castle says, looking Helen in the eyes, in the mirror.

'Like it is now,' Helen says in a strange, small voice, 'but half as long. Just above the shoulder.'

There is no small talk. The assistant has come back with Helen's cup of tea and put it on the little side table. Helen doesn't touch it.

She's too busy thinking she might be sick.

She counts to ten. She counts to a hundred. She counts to a million. She crawls into a sagging ketchup-stained bed with Ethan Hawke and William or Will and that squat little man with the beard from her last shoot. She gets prodded and poked with cheap camcorders and high-heeled shoes.

Helen doesn't feel like Helen any more.

She's Clair.

She's pretty sure that if she takes off her black smock thing, she'll be wearing her old school uniform underneath.

A clump of wet hair lands in her lap.

She is going to puke in front of Laura Castle and have to watch herself do it in the mirror.

She excuses herself. She says something vague, making it sound like she had a rough one last night, and Laura Castle has to stop cutting her hair and help her out of the chair and direct her to the toilet in the back.

A little round mirror hangs from a hook on the toilet door. Clair looks into it. Her hair is short on one side and still long on the other. She looks like a bad joke. The sick feeling has gone now but she sits on the lid with her head in her hands. Laura Castle and Jodie Salmon and all those other snooty stuck-up bitches at King's High never had anything whispered about *them* in the changing rooms after PE. Most of the rumours weren't even true.

She closes her eyes and feels something quiet and warm touch her on the cheek. She opens her eyes. It's the sister. The sister is speaking in sign language which Clair is somehow able to understand.

The sister tells Clair not to worry. She is an *actress*. Laura Castle is just some *poxy hairdresser* and, if this *is* a competition, if that's how she wants to look at it – which of course she shouldn't, but Christ does it feel like it sometimes – then Helen, who is not Clair anymore, has won. Helen is an actress and she is going to be a great one, the best.

Helen says 'Thank you' in sign language to the sister.

The sister signs 'Don't worry' and then 'Laura Castle's a cock'.

It makes Helen laugh.

She flushes the toilet. She walks back to the chair and sits down, feeling icy and impenetrable.

Laura Castle finishes the haircut with sharp steely snips, not saying anything. Then she gets out the hairdryer, and Helen breathes out and looks at herself.

It's over.

She swallows calmly, nods at the mirrored version of herself and says thanks to the hairdresser. She walks over to the till to pay. She gets out the three notes and checks to see if she has the 50p. When she finds she doesn't, she hands over an extra fiver. As she's waiting for the change her eyes drift to the floor. A tiny feeling – something about the size of a coin – swells then deflates inside her. The floor is littered with thousands and thousands of little black hairs that could each be the pube of a strange man in a weird empty house somewhere.

I am dyeing my hair black, Helen tells herself. I am dyeing my hair black because I feel like a change. I am dyeing my hair black to look like the winter.

She's sitting on a kitchen chair, wrapped in a towel, eating a cold slice of that pizza from the fridge, a plastic bag over her head.

I could go on holiday.

I could spend the money on a car and drive it into a rainforest.

I could live in the back of it and eat small flowers and drink out of ponds.

Corrine is out again at the casino.

Corrine has never asked Helen a question. Not really. When Corrine says, 'How are you?' or 'How was your day?' it's not a real question. It's just a sound; a kind of protection against silence and awkwardness. A statement: 'I am not going to be awkward around you. You make me feel awkward and uncomfortable. Fuck you.'

By the morning Helen still hasn't decided anything. When she gets on the bus it just happens to be going in the direction of his house. Plus, she needs the money. The rent is due next Monday.

She's taken out her contact lenses.

She presses her forehead against the window and feels the buzz of the wheels in her cheeks and smells the grit of old burnt plastic in her nose. She imagines herself sitting on that sofa of his in the living room and not smoking and him in silence, looking at her. He gets her to tell the Darren story again. He moves towards her and puts his cold empty hand on her cheek and whispers something beautiful and unexpected in her ear.

She does not imagine anything dangerous happening to her, as out of the bus window she sees nothing and nothing and nothing much zip past again and again and again.

Helen is wearing black heels, black tights, a black skirt, top and jacket. She has moistened her lips with her tongue and pressed the doorbell, and the door is swinging open and he is stood there in the gloom of the hall, looking older than he did last week, a lot older than seven days. His skin is grey and his eyes are sunken and his cheeks are hollowed. But maybe it's just that he's standing in the shadows and if he takes a step out onto the path he'll look clean and young and how she's kind of made him in her head since the first afternoon.

'Come in,' he says.

She walks past him into the hall and he closes the door behind her. She was expecting something else, she doesn't know what. Something more. Something kinder? It's very cold in here. Cold and impersonal, like coins in a till.

'This way,' he says.

She follows him up the stairs and into the bedroom. He's walking strangely, slightly hunched over. He wears jeans and a T-shirt. The hair on the nape of his neck is curly. Helen imagines taking all the clothes off him and laying him out on a patio in blazing sunshine and letting him cook. He's very white. He'd sizzle like bacon.

Like the other rooms, the bedroom is bare. Just a bed. The bed linen looks new, still scored with sharp creases from the packet. A cheap-looking hand-held video camera lies on top. There are a few clothes, too, folded neatly into squares and stacked in a pile.

'Right then,' she says, smiling awkwardly and looking at him, not knowing what else to say.

'Put these on,' he says, handing her the pile of clothes. 'Do it in the bathroom.'

Helen takes the pile of clothes. She goes into the bathroom. She locks the door, feeling silly but doing it anyway. She takes off her own clothes, folds them and puts them on top of the toilet.

The clothes he's given her are not things Helen would normally wear; a pair of blue jeans, a black vest top, a cardigan. There's even a pair of little black knickers and a pair of grey socks and a bra. Helen feels odd at first, putting them on, but the clothes themselves don't feel weird. They're the same size, exactly. They feel like her clothes, maybe, but from the future.

She wishes there was a mirror in here. She'd like one final look at herself before she goes back into the bedroom. She still isn't nervous. She imagines what she must look like; the black hair, Clair's eyes, the clothes of someone else.

Helen is an actress. She acts slight fear, making her heart beat a bit faster, making her breathing shallow. She unlocks the door and goes back into the bedroom.

William or Will is sitting on the bed. He looks up. Something changes in his face, like a drop of lemon juice has been dropped on it.

'Okay,' he says. 'Good.'

'What do you want me to do?' she says.

He gets up off the bed, takes off his T-shirt, unbuckles his belt and steps out of his jeans. His penis springs out of his trousers. It looks very hard and red. She thinks she can hear a buzzing sound. Maybe it's coming from the camera he's holding now and pointing at her. She hears the beep. She sees the red light come on.

'Take off your clothes,' he says.

He walks around her, behind her, so she can see him in the dresser mirror. He films her from behind as she begins to unbutton the cardigan, unclip the bra, shuffle out of the jeans.

In the mirror, she stares into the gaping glass eye of the lens.

Inside she's shivering.

She steps out of the knickers, then feels his cold hand on her shoulder. He turns her to face him.

Helen and Clair feel very beautiful.

I hereby give the bearer of this note written permission to do whatever the hell he likes to me . . .

Will has the note now. He must do. I've looked everywhere. It's gone. He took it. Maybe Alice slipped it to him under the table. I can see us walking off down the street; Will waving goodbye, leant against a streetlamp.

Once we've turned the corner, he takes the little square of paper out of his pocket and unfolds it.

He reads it.

He licks his lips.

He reads it a second time.

. . . and I promise I won't mind. In fact, I'll probably like it quite a lot.

His mouth curls into a lewd budgie-eating grin.

I still have his spare key.

It's hard to tell if Will's home. The curtains are drawn. I knock on the door and wait.

I knock again.

Nothing.

I slide the key into the lock and turn it slowly. The door clicks open. I stick my head into the hall. The roll-up and aftershave smell. Darkness. Silence. I let myself in and close the door softly behind me, treading on a pile of bills and circulars, leaving wet footprints on them. Fuck it.

I start in the living room, going through the drawers and the mess of paper and things on the coffee table. A cut-out from a newspaper supplement. 'Cheep tricks' the caption reads. A puff piece. A photo of the exhibition and another of Will, leering at the camera, his arms folded. Unopened gas bills and telephone bills with shopping lists written on the back (BREAD, MARGE, LIGHTBULBS, CONDOMS?). But no note.

In the bedroom I try to remember what colour jeans he was wearing the night we met. I go through the pockets of the pairs strewn around the floor and hanging off the end of the bed. Just receipts, bits of fluff, loose change and about eight ten-pound notes. I pocket three.

Under the bed, an old leather suitcase, brown and scuffed. I pull it out. A combination lock. I shuffle the numbers, randomly. *Click, click, click.* I imagine the note in there, lying innocently next to a bottle of baby lotion, a whip and a huge purple dildo. I try more combinations. *Click, click, click.*

I can see Alice, lying back on his tiger-print bedspread, pulling off her knickers, her legs in the air. Will is taking photos. His camera flashes. Alice. The note. Will doing whatever the hell he likes to her and Alice not minding, probably liking it quite a lot.

I hear a key in the lock downstairs and my heart lurches. The front door opens then slams. I push the suitcase under the bed, stand up and look round frantically. If this were a film there'd be a big empty wardrobe to hide in. But all Will uses is an old waist-high dresser and the floor.

'Hello?' Will's voice.

If he comes up the stairs, I'll hide behind the door. I'll use that radio alarm clock thing next to the bed to smash him over the head.

He walks down the hall and turns on the light.

I could break down in tears. Confess. Tell him about the note and how everything's been going wrong with me and Alice lately, and how ('So stupid of me, really . . . ridiculous . . .') I've suspected something's going on between them.

He's put the kettle on. I hear more walking sounds, the telly going on in the living room, Will whistling to himself.

Then a foot on the stairs.

I hold my breath.

He's coming this way.

Oh, Christ.

He's coming up the stairs.

I move behind the door and try to pick up the radio alarm clock, but it's plugged in at the wall. The cord pulls tight.

He's on the landing now. A door opens, then closes with a click. The bathroom. Thank fuck. He's in the bathroom. I hear the jingle of his belt, the zip of his flies and the heavy manly *sloosh* of his piss.

I tread quietly onto the landing and down the stairs.

The toilet flushes.

I run the rest of the way, fumbling with the latch at the front door, finally getting it open, letting it close softly behind me. I breathe in the cold wet air outside. Spots of rain land on my cheeks, feeling like pieces of hot glass.

I'm halfway down the path.

I turn back.

I knock on the door.

Will opens it, still buckling his belt. He squints at me. He looks like he was expecting someone else.

'Alright,' he says. There's something shifty in the way he says it, something suspicious.

'I still have your spare key,' I say, and hand it to him.

'Cheers,' he says. 'Want to come in for a drink?' He doesn't look me in the eye. He looks at the floor.

'No, thanks,' I say. 'Listen, Will. You didn't *find* anything the other week, when we went for dinner, did you?'

'How d'you mean?' he says. He puts his hand in his

pocket. The left one. He shuffles his weight from one foot to the other. He looks at me funny. I bet he's got it on him.

'Just that when I emptied out my wallet at the restaurant, I think I lost something.'

'What?' he says. 'Like a cash card?'

'Yeah. Something like that.'

'Nah, didn't notice anything.'

'Alright. Never mind.'

'Hey,' he calls, as I'm turning into the street. 'You're still coming round for dinner sometime, right?'

I pretend I haven't heard.

We get in a bit drunk and heat up some leftovers.

'It's not going too well, is it?' Alice says.

The 'it' she's referring to is us.

'What isn't?' I ask.

She drops her fork on her plate, stands up and starts scraping stuff into the bin. I hear the hiss of *fuck's sake* under her breath. She rinses her plate. She turns and looks at me. She leans against the kitchen counter. She's wearing the long black jumper, the one that covers her neck and hangs down past her knuckles.

'What do you think?' she says.

'I don't know,' I say.

(I know exactly what she's talking about.)

'Christ,' she says and storms out of the kitchen.

I wait for the sound of things being thrown into

boxes, things being lugged down stairs, things being smashed against a wall. If she leaves, I can't afford to live here any more, not without getting a job. If she leaves, I don't know what I'll do. I hear the TV being turned on in the living room and the closing music of some programme. I go through. She's on the sofa.

'Cup of tea?' I ask.

'A cup of tea isn't going to solve anything,' she says. She puts her hand on top of her head. 'William, in case you didn't notice, we just sat in that bloody pub for about two hours and said pretty much nothing to each other. We've become one of those sad old couples you see. It's awful. I want to talk to you.'

Alice paid for all the drinks.

I don't know what to say. I feel frozen. I feel like a display model of a human being. Things have gone so far past okay, I don't know what to do. I don't want to talk about it. I want to pretend everything's fine. I want to somehow not be here any more; to not be the cause of the problem. I want Alice to carry on happily in the house without me, until I somehow sort myself out. If I had money, I'd book a holiday. France. The moon. Give her space. And then, after a while, I'll come back, and she'll put her arms around me and kiss me on the head and tell me how much she's missed me.

Or I could get a job.

(I won't get a job.)

I go into the kitchen and fill the kettle. I wait for it to boil. I look through the window at where the back yard should be and there's just blackness. I can imagine Alice looking at me sometimes, too, and where I should be there's nothing.

I make two cups of tea. I carry them through. I put one next to her foot. I wait for her to touch it. There's a gardening programme on. She reaches down to her ankle and I think she's going to pick it up. I get excited. I wait for her to pick up the mug. If she picks up the mug, I think, then she is still in love with me and everything's going to be okay. But she just scratches her leg and folds her hands back in her lap.

It's two days later, or three, or four. The evenings have become as cold and small as marbles. We aren't talking. Alice turns off the TV halfway through a programme. She looks at me instead of the TV. Her eyes are wet. She's about to cry.

'We need to have a talk,' she says. Her voice is low and quiet.

I'm scared of what's coming next. I look at the TV instead of her.

'What is it you do all day again?' she says.

Here it comes. The end. She's found me out.

'I went on your computer,' she says.

I want to pull my T-shirt over my head. I want to hide in it until she's finished.

'And there weren't any of those bloody spreadsheets

you always go on about, as far as I could see. All I could see was a load of porn saved on the hard drive.'

I look at the floor, at the TV, at my hand, at anything but her. I look at a flake of Rich Tea biscuit on the carpet.

'Right. So you're not even speaking to me now, is that it?'

'I don't know what to say,' I say.

She stands up.

She sits down again.

She touches her hair, wrapping a piece of it round her neck.

'Look, I don't mind if you want to look at porn all day. That's your business. It just seems . . . I don't know. Why didn't you tell me the truth? I feel like I don't even know you sometimes. It scares me. Do you know what I mean?'

I could get angry here. I could say, 'Well, why didn't you feel you could tell me the truth about your parents?'

'Why did you have to lie to me?' she says. 'That's what I don't understand. I wouldn't have been mad if you didn't have a job. That's not why I liked you . . .'

Liked, I think. Past tense.

I could say, I am looking for that film of you. I want to find it and destroy it. I think about it all day every day.

I could say, Why did you do it? Why did you make it? Did it turn you on? Did you hate yourself afterwards? Did you do it *because* you hated yourself?

I could say, What about Will? What's going on there? You want to fuck him, don't you?

Or, Why do you even stay with me? I don't understand it. I do nothing. I don't even talk. It must be like living with a ghost.

I could say, Do you even love me any more?

But I say nothing.

'How about you?' she says. 'Anything you want to ask me?'

She stands up again. She waits for me to speak. I don't speak.

'Fuck it. We can't go on like this. It's ridiculous. I'm sure if we *talked* about things we could try and sort it out, but it looks like we can't even do that any more.'

She's in the doorway. The phone's ringing. I don't care if it's my parents. Pick it up, Alice. Introduce yourself. Explain that you're my girlfriend (soon to be ex-) and ask them how they are. Talk about the weather.

She sniffs. She rubs her face with her palm. I want to be her palm. I want to rub her face and make her feel better. I can't move. She walks into the hall. She picks up the phone.

'Hello?'

Pause.

I hear her laugh.

'Oh, hello,' she's saying.

She laughs again.

I don't believe it.

I turn the telly back on.

Only one person could make her laugh like that and I know exactly what he's saying. There's nothing I can do to stop him.

A few minutes later she reappears in the doorway.

'In case you were wondering,' she says, 'that was Will. He's invited us round to his for dinner, a week on Friday, and I've accepted.'

Great.

'Come if you want,' she says. 'But I'm going, anyway.'

I've put some of my things on eBay; about one hundred CDs, two thirds of my books, a lamp, my guitar. I have an old watch, too, that belonged to my granddad.

I want to put myself on eBay.

I want to sell myself to the highest bidder.

I will give Alice all the money I make from selling myself on eBay. I will put it in an envelope with just the word SORRY written on it. I will leave it on the kitchen table, then post myself.

'You currently have no bidders.'

I've done nothing today, not even turned on the computer or opened the curtains.

When Alice gets home from work, she finds me lying on the sofa. I've been drinking red wine. My teeth are grey. She leans over and kisses me lightly on the forehead. Her hair brushes my face.

'Happy birthday,' she says.

I move myself into a sitting position.

'Thanks,' I say.

She kneels down in front of me. She puts her hands on my knees.

She moves one of the hands up and down my thigh.

Her eyes are sad-looking.

I want to say, 'I'm sorry.'

I want to tell her about the things I've put on eBay.

It doesn't seem like the right time.

The hand moves to my crotch. It massages my crotch. It unbuckles my belt. It unzips my jeans. I can't look her in the eyes. I look at the top of her head instead, as it lowers towards my lap. I put one of my hands on her head. I don't know what to do with the hand so I just sort of rest it there on top of her head. She tugs at my jeans. I lift myself off the sofa, so she can pull my jeans and boxers down over my knees. My penis is limp. It looks very small. We both look down at it. I've not had an erection now in over a week, maybe two. Not since I lost the note.

She puts my penis in her mouth.

I try to imagine I'm watching this on the computer, that this is a free preview clip I've downloaded from some amateur ex-girlfriend site.

I feel nothing.

She takes my penis out of her mouth.

It's still small. Small and wet and cold.

'I'm sorry,' I say.

'What do you want me to do?' she says.

A tear is crawling down her face.

'I want you to ignore me,' I say. 'I want you to ignore me completely.'

The tear stops moving. It freezes halfway down her cheek.

'Okay,' she says, and a sheet of something falls heavily and definitely between us.

The alarm wakes us up as usual. 8.15. Alice reaches across me to turn it off. Her arm manages not to touch me as she does this. She sits up and brushes hair from her face.

'Are you still ignoring me?' I say.

She licks something from the corner of her mouth and breathes in deeply. She's still half-asleep. Light from the window is tangling in her hair.

She's not looked at me yet.

She's looked in my direction, but not at me.

'Well?' I say. My voice sounds like a piece of wet string.

She lifts herself out of bed and walks to the wardrobe. There's a small blue bruise on the back of her thigh in the shape of a horse's head. She opens the wardrobe and takes out some clothes. I watch the bruise disappear beneath her grey work skirt. She unbuttons the shirt she sleeps in and throws it onto the bed.

The warm sleepy smell of her comes from it. It comes out of the shirt and upwards towards my nose, but doesn't go into my nostrils.

Even the smell of her is ignoring me.

She fastens her bra and buttons up her work blouse.

She goes into the bathroom and turns on the tap. She brushes her teeth and spits in the sink. She goes downstairs and finds her keys. She opens the front door, then closes it.

I lie in bed a long time, staying on my side of it, making sure I don't touch the pillow she's been sleeping on.

I get up and put on my dressing gown.

I have a piss.

I go into the empty spare bedroom and turn on the computer. No new emails. I look at the things I'm selling on eBay; three bidders for the lamp, seventeen for the guitar and some of the CDs have sold. Then I download porn; any clip I can find with the description 'amateur British girlfriend'. None of them is her. With each new clip I watch, it feels like something inside my brain is being sanded away. I check my emails again. Still nothing. I don't know what I'm expecting to find. I check my spam mail: 'You have 400 new messages.'

Two hundred for penis enlargement.

One hundred and ninety nine for Viagra.

One for discount golfing equipment.

I think of Barry and all those other old blokes down the pub. I wonder if they still have that scam going with dodgy knock-off Viagra. The first time I met Barry, he tried to sell me some 'Vs' in the pub toilet. I said I was alright. He said if I ever changed my mind I should give him a call and stuck a stained little business card in my pocket:

Barry Turner – Garden Solutions

'Planting, mowing and everything in between.'

(tel:) 0779 664 6645

I go into the bedroom. I take my jeans off the back of the chair and empty the contents of my wallet onto the dresser table. Will may have that note she wrote me, but Barry's card is exactly where I left it.

Friday night. Her long black coat is gone from the hook. She's out. She's at Will's. She's not coming home. Three in the morning. I'm lying on the floor in the hall by the front door like a rug. She'll have to step on me when she gets in. She will wipe her feet on me.

I watched her get ready. I stood behind her as she put on her make-up in the bathroom mirror. I followed her into the bedroom and watched her open the wardrobe and take out three different dresses, all black. She held them up against her body and swayed from side to side, watching herself in the dresser mirror. She chose the shortest one. She put on a pair of earrings, sprayed herself with perfume and used straightening irons on her hair. It took her an hour and a half. She listened to Erasure and then to Prince. She sang along.

'I wanna be your lover.'

I sat on the bed and watched her get ready. I didn't say anything.

Now I'm lying on the floor in the hall, watching the crack under the front door, waiting for it to turn from black to blue or for Alice to come in and find me, whichever comes first.

I won't fall asleep, I tell myself.

When I wake up there's a free newspaper lying on my leg. The crack is letting in bright white sunlight. It hurts my eyes.

I squint at the coat rack.

Her coat is hanging from the hook.

Her boots are back by the door.

She's in the shower. I can hear her. She's singing.

There's this group of lads that hang around the top of our street once it gets dark. I used to pass them on my way home from work. They sit on the wall and smoke fags and swig from big blue bottles of cider. They're terrifying. They watch you walk past and think about the different ways they could mug you.

I'm on my way to the post office. I have to post our toaster to a man in Cardiff. The hat stand in the corner of the living room is now up to seventeen bids on eBay. The coffee table is at twenty-four. I've not sold my granddad's watch yet, even though it's the most expensive thing I own. It's a last resort. I imagine selling the watch on eBay and making maybe six hundred pounds and then my parents coming round on a surprise visit. They come round on the anniversary of my granddad's death. We talk about my granddad and then they ask to see the watch. They sit in the living room as I go upstairs and pretend to look for it, forever.

The lads watch me walk past. They eye up the parcel under my arm.

Alice was out again last night. She's begun to smell different, of roll-ups and aftershave. She's begun singing different songs in the shower, too; ones I haven't heard.

'Alright, mate,' says one of the lads.

'Fucking pansy,' says another.

They jeer and shout as I scurry off down the street, and I feel something small and hard ping off the back of my head, a stone or a bottle top.

Being ignored was a bad idea. It hasn't helped. I feel worse. I feel redundant. I'm beginning to wonder if I still exist.

I want to do something dramatic.

I want Alice to see me again.

I want none of this to have happened.

Speaking doesn't work.

Maybe I'll get a tattoo on my face, of the words I LOVE YOU and I'M SORRY.

At the post office, cashier number four is bored and glassy-eyed. I put my parcel on the scales and ask for second-class postage to Cardiff. Cashier number four doesn't speak. I have to look over at the till display to find out the price.

I've not spoken to anyone in over a week. My tongue is the colour of something rusting.

I put the correct amount down on the counter. The cashier takes the money. He prints out a label and sticks it to my parcel. He presses a button and a computer voice says, 'Next customer to cashier number four, please.'

According to my receipt it's just gone five. Alice should be home from work soon, unless she's out again with Will.

If the lads are still there on the way back, I'm going to say something offensive to them. I'm going to take their big blue bottle of cider and throw it into the street.

The lads will beat me up. They will kick my fucking face in. They'll stamp on my knees and boot me in the ribs and leave me lying on the pavement with my face swollen and bloody and some of my teeth missing.

I will pick myself up and hobble home. Alice will be in the kitchen eating dinner. She'll look over at me when I come in, her fork frozen inches from her mouth.

'Oh, my god,' she'll say, her mouth opening wider and the fork falling onto her plate. 'Oh, my god. You poor darling. What happened?'

She'll stand up and come towards me.

She'll reach out her hands to stroke my face softly and carefully.

Then she will begin to cry.

* * *

The lads are still sat on the wall on my way back, passing the bottle of cider between them and smoking fags. They have their hoods up. It's spotting with rain.

When I get close to them I stop.

They look at me.

'What do you want?' one of them says, putting the bottle down on the wall.

'Yeah?' says another.

'Do you want to bum us, mate?' says a third.

I reach for the bottle of cider.

'Oi!' says one of the lads.

He jumps down from the wall and pushes me backwards. Something jars sharply in my spine. I feel scared. I turn and run, hearing the sound of the lads clattering down the street behind me.

'Fucking get him!' one of them shouts.

'Yeah!' shout the others.

I outrun them. I am propelled down the street by the fear of getting hit.

I reach my door and fumble with the key. I get it open, slam it behind me and peer out through the spyhole. The lads are gathering at the end of the path. They don't know what to do. A couple of them spit at the house and throw empty cans and stick up their fingers. It's raining heavily now. After a while they drift away.

Alice is in the kitchen, eating a bowl of cornflakes for dinner. I sit down opposite.

'I almost got beaten up by those lads at the end of our street,' I say.

She lifts a spoonful of cornflakes up to her mouth.

'I just posted our toaster to a man in Cardiff,' I say.

She lifts another spoonful of cornflakes up to her mouth.

'Sometimes I wonder if I still exist,' I say.

I get up and go into the bathroom. I look at myself in the mirror. I bare my teeth. I stick out my tongue. I put my hands on top of my head. I've not had a proper conversation with anyone now in over a week.

I open the phonebook in the hall and dial a number.

'Good evening, Dixons,' says the voice on the other end, clear and professional.

'Oh, yes,' I say. 'I'm thinking about buying a widescreen TV. I was wondering which one you'd recommend . . .'

The voice begins to list widescreen TVs. It tells me about their various merits and prices.

I listen for a while. Then, very softly, I rest the receiver on the phone table and walk away.

She's put candles on the table. Two placemats are arranged, next to two knives, two forks, two soup-spoons. She's tied up her hair. She's put on a necklace. She's wearing the short black dress again. The oven is humming. The smell of meat and sauces comes from it. A pan of home-made soup simmers on the stove. Alice skitters from the table to the oven, then over to the fridge. She takes out a bottle of red wine. This is how they do it in the London bars, she's heard him say. They refrigerate it.

She puts the bottle on the table and adjusts the wine glasses next to it.

She's not wearing a bra.

She seems nervous and excited.

I'm not dressed for the occasion. I'm not wearing any socks. I have day-old ketchup down the front of my shirt.

She lights the candles and turns off the light. Then she stands back and smiles to herself.

She is blowing out the candles and turning the light back on when the doorbell rings.

She runs to answer it.

'Come in,' I hear her say.

Then Will's voice. 'You look great.'

The door closes. She is taking his coat and hanging it up. Will is kicking off his shoes. A sound like a kiss.

I look at the pan of soup on the hob. I could pour it down the sink. I could take out whatever's cooking in the oven and boot it into the yard. I could pour the bottle of wine over my head and stick the candles up my nose and drop the glasses on the floor.

'Come through,' she says, leading him up the hall. 'Sorry about the mess. I'm a bit disorganised. Oh, wait here . . .'

She runs through and lights the candles, then turns off the light.

'Okay,' she calls. 'Ready.'

Will has to duck to get through the doorway. He sees me straight away. He gives me a weak surprised smile then looks down at his shoes.

'Alright, mate,' he mumbles. 'Didn't know you were . . .'

'Sit down, sit down,' Alice says. 'It's almost ready.'

Will takes the space facing the oven. He watches her back as she pours soup into our two fanciest bowls.

Then he looks over at me, fiddling with the stem of his glass.

'So,' he says.

'It's carrot and red pepper,' she says, putting the bowls of soup on the table. 'Wine?'

'Sure,' he says, taking the bottle and pouring it.

I sit down at the empty end of the table.

'Are you . . . erm . . .' says Will in my direction.

'Right,' she says, scraping her chair as she sits down. Then she smiles at him. 'I'm so glad you came over.'

I feel something cold brush my leg. I shuffle back in my seat and look at it under the table. It's her foot. She's placed it on top of Will's foot.

'Thanks for inviting me,' says Will. He's relaxing a bit. He's cocking his head and grinning at her.

I stand up quickly. My chair falls over.

I go into the living room and turn on the telly.

I sit down on the sofa and flick through the channels.

They laugh at something.

I turn up the volume.

They laugh again. 'Ha, ha, ha!'

I turn off the TV.

I go through and take my place at the table, picking up my chair and sitting in it.

'Nice, um, soup,' says Will, eyeing me.

His brow is furrowed.

His hands look big and stupid.

I take the wine bottle from the table and pour the remaining third over my head.

Alice starts clearing the bowls away and then serves the main course. It's chicken. She's using my favourite plates; my ones from uni with the paintings of Italy on them.

'Those are my plates,' I say when she puts them on the table.

'They're nice plates,' says Will, uncovering some of the design with his fork. 'Italy,' he says, nodding at it.

'Go on,' she says. 'Start.'

'I'm not sure,' he says, looking over at me again.

'What's wrong?' she says. 'Don't you like chicken?'

'It's not that,' he says. 'It's just . . .' He nods my way.

'It's *what?*' she says sharply, her face souring.

'Nothing,' he says and lifts a forkful to his mouth.

They begin to eat. Will compliments her on her cooking. She reaches over and puts her hand on top of his, brushing his big stupid fingers with her thumb. Her eyes are sparkling again. Will tells her about work, how he's taken on this important new commission. The London exhibition really boosted his profile. He's selling more than ever, and if things keep going the way they're going he might even be able to move.

'Wonderful,' she says.

She's imagining herself moving in with him, becoming the wife of the great artist. In her head she's stretched out naked on a white sheet and Will is painting her, permanently capturing her beauty.

They make a lot of noise when they eat. They smack their lips and talk through their food.

Will opens another bottle of wine. He clenches the bottle between his thighs, straining and grunting, and Alice watches him lovingly, twirling a strand of hair between her fingers. The cork comes out with a loud plop. A bit of wine spills onto the lino.

They finish their meals. She clears the plates away. They stay at the table, talking. They finish the second bottle. She offers him coffee but he asks if there's any more alcohol and she comes back with a bottle of vodka and two tumblers. My tumblers.

'Cheers.'

'Salut.'

'Let's move through to the other room,' she says, 'where it's more comfortable. No, no, don't bother clearing away. I'll do it later.'

Alice totters slightly when she stands. She lets herself fall against him, throwing her arm around his waist as if to steady herself.

'Whoops,' he says. 'I've got you.'

She doesn't move her arm away.

I follow them into the living room.

Will sits on the sofa, holding his drink. Alice is in front of him, dancing. No music is playing. She holds out her hands. He puts the glass down by his foot. He stands up. He takes her hands and puts them around his back. She rests her head on his shoulder.

They turn slowly.

His hands are on her back.

They turn.

His hands are on her back.

They turn again.

His hands are on her arse.

They stop dancing. They're kissing now.

His hands are in her hair.

Her leg is thrust between his.

Her shoe is hanging off her foot.

She is biting his ear.

Will leans over and kisses her shoulder. Then he stops, some of her hair caught in the stubble on his chin, and looks at me in the doorway.

'But what about . . .' he says.

'What *is* it?' she says.

'I don't know if I can do this.'

'Sure you can. Come here.'

She holds his head in her hands, blinkering him. She pulls him close and winds herself around him.

Then they fuck.

I got the message this evening:

Vs sortd. Meet u in Noose bogs 10.30.

I'm loitering by the urinals, not making eye contact and pretending to wash my hands every time someone comes in. I've washed them six times now. Barry is late. My fingers are starting to sting.

Today is Tuesday. Tuesday is *Pub Quiz Nite!* Muffled questions and cheers leak in through the crack of the door. Whenever it opens and closes, the air displacement makes the sinks rattle.

I feel shifty.

I am sober.

I'm not here to look at nobs.

A big drunk man comes in; Borstal tattoos, sovereign rings, a front tooth missing.

I pretend to finish zipping up and go over to the sinks. I wash my hands for the seventh time. I can't feel the soap anymore.

The urinals flush in unison. They mock me with a chorus of gurgling disinfectant.

She fucked him, she fucked him, she fucked him, she fucked him.

The big drunk bloke is washing his hands now. I'm stripping the skin off my knuckles at the drier; the hot air is like sandpaper.

Where's Barry? Good old Barry, with all those burst capillaries winding around his nose like a driving map of the Yorkshire Dales.

Now the drunk bloke is after the drier, so I shuffle over to the mirror, touching my hair and waiting for him to leave. I'd hide in the cubicle but someone's kicked the door in and shat on it. It's one of those pub mirrors which is nothing more than a square of scrubbed semi-reflective metal bolted to the wall.

She fucked him, she fucked him, she fucked him, she fucked him.

The bloke leaves and the door closes.

Her coat was gone from the hook by the door. Her big brown boots were missing, too. She's out with him again. They're in public somewhere, fucking. Market Square, probably. A crowd has gathered. Someone is handing out balloons and commemorative plates. A group of tourists is clapping and taking photographs.

The drier stops.

I get back into position with my fly halfway unzipped at the far left urinal.

Someone has written

Why can't the world be tender and kind?

on the tiles in marker pen.

Underneath it, someone else has written

FUCK YOU

Barry comes in.

'Fuck, mate, sorry,' he says. 'You wouldn't believe the night I've had.'

Barry's right. I don't believe the night he's had. He tells me some long-winded story about this 'German tart' that he's 'banging on the side'.

I only half-listen.

I can't look him in the eyes.

He finally rustles around in the pocket of his tweed jacket and comes out with a boiled sweet, two raffle tickets and a little plastic container, for camera film. He hands it over. Something rattles inside.

She fucked him, she fucked him, she's fucking him now.

'No shame in it, lad,' he says. 'Neck one of these bastards and you'll be chopping wood with your bell-end. Rock solid, I guarantee it.'

I open the lid of the container and shake the pills onto my palm. They are a pale oval blue. There are four of them.

'I only need the one,' I say.

I am not a man. I am a hat stand.

I'm standing in the corner of the living room, naked. Her favourite hat hangs from my erection. It's getting cold. I've been here too long.

I hear a key in the lock and then her boots in the hall, clipping this way.

She turns on the light and pauses in the doorway. She looks around the room, but not in my direction. Then she turns and walks through to the kitchen. I hear her begin to whistle. I take off the beret. My penis is so hard it's almost making a noise.

She's in the kitchen.

She's making instant coffee.

I sidle up behind her. My penis accidentally knocks the saltshaker off the dinner table on the way. It smashes on the tiles. She doesn't even blink.

She pours hot water into a mug and stirs it with a spoon. She turns and walks past me. A faint smell of roll-up cigarettes.

I look at my reflection in the back-door window.

I'm still here. I still exist.

I hear the TV go on in the other room and the clatter of something far away, like a cat falling off a fence. I hear the hiss of my breath. And something else, too. A small humming noise. I bend down. It's coming from my dick – a buzzing sound, like a wasp trapped in a pint glass.

I stand in the doorway.

'Alice,' I say, 'I've made a mistake. I don't want you to ignore me any more.'

She sips her coffee.

'I'll do anything,' I say.

She puts the mug down by her foot and scratches her nose. She blows a strand of hair from her face.

'Just tell me and I'll do it.'

I stand in the doorway for the length of a chat show. The buzzing from my penis becomes so loud it fills the room and rattles the windows. She must be able to hear it. I ask her again and again, What is it you want me to do?

Then I know.

I know now what she wants.

Eventually she yawns and switches off the TV. She

turns off the light. I follow her along the hall and up the stairs and into the bedroom. She's in front of the mirror, unbuttoning her cardigan, pulling off her vest, unclipping her bra, wriggling out of her jeans. Behind her, in the mirror, my eyes are wide and black. She steps out of her knickers. I watch my hand come up behind her. I watch it touch her shoulder. I'd almost forgotten what her skin feels like. It's smooth and soft and ice cold. She doesn't flinch or pull away. She doesn't do anything. I look into her eyes in the mirror. I turn her to face me.

My dick buzzes loudly between us.

Alice picks her way quietly round the room. The morning; too late for her to make it into work today. The alarm clock didn't go off because it's in the post to a woman in Portsmouth. Her legs are slightly bruised. Her hair falls in her face as she untangles a pair of knickers from the pile of clothes at the foot of the bed. They go on first. Goodbye, vagina.

I lie on my back, watching her dress. She clasps the bra around her waist, slips it up over her breasts. I see the white knots of her spine. I see her nipples in the dresser mirror. I watch them disappear into the cups of the bra. Goodbye, left nipple. Goodbye, right.

Then there is her mouth, broken by slivers of hair. No speaking sound comes from it. She covers her arms and shoulders with the cardigan. Her belly disappears, button by button. Her fingers shake. I watch the denim of her jeans swallow the chicken-leg birthmark on her thigh.

Goodbye, knee, elbow, ankle and arse.

Goodbye, collarbone, contacts and calf muscle.

Goodbye, goosebump.

Once she's fully disappeared, she goes about making the bed as though I'm not in it. She straightens the sheets, plumps the pillows, folds, brushes and tucks. I lie there like something wooden, unfeeling.

She's in the hall now, by the phone. I hear a jangle of keys, a clink of change and the beep of a new message received. I hear her zip up her boots, pocket her purse and clip four steps to the door. Finally, I hear the swish of traffic and trees.

After a while I get up. I don't get dressed. I go downstairs naked and stand in the hall by the phone. Her coat is gone. Her boots are gone. They aren't coming back this time.

She's left the front door open and I stand for a while in the doorway. A bright cold morning, the tarmac wet with dew. A car drives past. The driver looks at me funny, and he mutters something to himself. I walk down the path and stand on the pavement. A little kid in the distance shouts something. His mates point and laugh. Someone in the house across the road is watching from a bedroom window. I look up and down the street. Nothing. She's gone.

So I go back up the path and into the house and close the door behind me.

William pushes Helen backwards towards the bed. She lets herself flop onto it, feeling the cold starchy duvet against her back. She pulls her knees up and opens her legs. The curtains are drawn. The light in this room is cold and yellow and electric. He climbs onto the bed, positioning himself over her, awkwardly fumbling with a condom, tearing it open with his teeth and putting it on with his free hand, not letting go of the camera. He keeps the viewfinder firm against his eye. The camera obscures most of his face. She can just see his mouth, which is screwed closed, and his left eye, which is a slit.

Helen has done a lot of things in her job.

She's pissed into things, put things inside her, spoken all kinds of lewd pre-written things to camera.

But this will be the first time she's actually had sex for money.

Helen doesn't know what to do with her face. Usually, when she's being filmed, the camera will move down towards her body. It will zoom in on her breasts or her vagina, leaving her face free to do whatever it wants. Her face will become bored or mock-serious or real-serious or absent, and she will start to think of something like how she forgot to tape a programme for Corrine or what she'll say to her mum when she calls back later on.

But William hasn't taken the camera away from Helen's face. He hasn't panned it down to her body. She looks deep into the lens, watching it curl and open.

She tries to look how a 'desirable woman' might look.

She flutters her eyelashes.

She opens her mouth.

She licks her bottom lip with her tongue.

She lets her breath purr past her teeth in a seductive *oooh* sound.

The tip of his penis is centimetres away from her vagina. She's not used any kind of lubricant and she realises she's not wet. She puts her hand on her belly, slides it down towards her vagina, but then feels awkward and lets it drop to her side.

He's not moving the camera away from her face. The veins in his neck are standing out. There are wisps of hair on his chest. She thinks she can hear his heart beating.

Helen feels herself become completely static and, for the first time, imagines what will happen afterwards; him playing the tape back once she's gone, sat there in the dark with his hand down his trousers, watching her face as it arranges itself into a series of ridiculous porn star expressions.

She isn't nervous. She isn't nervous. Helen is an actress.

The tip of his penis is now millimetres from her vagina.

'Oooh,' she says, batting her eyelashes at the camera lens. 'Fuck me.'

He freezes.

'Please,' she says.

His penis is one millimetre from her vagina.

There is a beeping noise and the red record light blinks off.

He takes the camera from his face, pushes himself up into a sitting position and moves to the end of the bed, facing away from her. He puts the camera down next to him. He takes off the condom and rests his head in his hands. Helen can still see his penis, poking up from between his legs. It looks absurd, in contrast with the rest of his body which is pale and drooping, sad-looking.

'Did I do something wrong?' she says, not in the porno voice.

He shakes his head.

Helen knows she did something wrong, but can't work out what.

'It's impossible, anyway,' he says. 'What I was trying to do. It's impossible.'

'Oh,' says Helen. 'Okay.'

She wants to touch his back. She knows it will make no difference to anything whatsoever, but she really wants to reach out her hand and touch his back, and for him to know that she doesn't have to touch his back, that she doesn't have to do anything at all if she doesn't want to, but she's done it anyway.

She moves closer, waits a few seconds. He doesn't seem real. He seems like a parody of something or like he's been turned inside-out, and she feels bad that it's her seeing the inside things of him. She wants to tell him it's okay. She wants to tell him everyone's fucked up. She wants to tell him about some of the strange things people have made her do for money.

She reaches out her hand and touches his back.

He flinches.

He stands.

He turns to face her.

Helen looks at his penis, which is still incredibly hard and pointing at her face like an angry buzzing finger. It is making a noise.

Helen wants to laugh. She feels it mount inside her; a manic violent laughter like a pan of water, boiling then overflowing. She keeps her face blank but lets the laughter spill out silently inside her.

He notices her looking at his penis. He looks down at it, too.

'It's Viagra,' he says.

'Oh,' says Helen.

She looks up at his face.

The laughter turns from boiling water to salt. It falls in a dry shower on the pit of her stomach.

'How long does it last?' Helen asks.

'About twelve hours,' he says.

'Oh my god,' she says.

She can't help herself. She starts to laugh again, this time outwardly. She imagines him having to make dinner, brush his teeth, read a newspaper, all with that ridiculous throbbing hard-on.

'Doesn't it make it difficult? You know, if you want to go out or something?'

His expression changes; not a smile, but something, like the corner of a curtain being lifted back and a tiny bit of light getting in.

'I don't really get out that much,' he says, picking up his clothes.

When Helen was Clair – when she was about eight years old – her parents took her to a farm. One of those ones open to the public. There were other things there, too; go-carts, trampolines, a gift shop. It probably wasn't a real farm, one that actually produced anything. The animals were farmed to be touched. It was the summer holidays – a sunny day, now bleached sepia-yellow in Helen's memory.

'Go on,' her mum said.

They were looking at a sheep. The sheep was sniffing the fence or chewing a piece of grass.

Clair felt scared. She felt the sheep might do something weird and violent to her; bite off her face or smack her round the head with its hoof. She didn't really want to, but she walked towards the sheep, to please her mum.

Clair held out her hand. The sheep came over. It licked her hand and she felt the rough scrape of its tongue on her palm.

She felt surprised.

It was good, and she felt silly for feeling scared, and she wondered if there was some way you could be employed to do this; if this could be your job, to just stand there and have your palm licked all day.

Afterwards, she wanted to ask her mum. But even at eight years old she knew it was a silly thing to say out loud.

It's dark when Helen comes out of his house. She steps carefully past the snails and out onto the street. It's raining still. He gave her the money in an envelope, which she hasn't opened yet. There's nothing written on the front of it.

She went back into the bathroom and put on her own clothes.

She had to keep suppressing the urge to talk to him more, to ask him if there was anything she could do, like if he needed anything from the shops or whatever. Of course, she didn't ask. She felt silly. She didn't lock the bathroom door. She kept trying to imagine what he wanted her to look like. She had to stop herself about five times from going back into the bedroom and saying, Let's give it another try.

What the fuck are you doing? she asked herself, rolling her tights up over her legs.

'You can have these if you like,' he said when she went back into the bedroom.

He handed her a carrier bag; the clothes she'd been wearing.

She didn't know whether she wanted them or not, but she said thanks anyway and smiled at him. He must have sensed she felt weird, because he said, 'You could give them to a charity shop or something.'

'Right,' she said.

Then he gave her the envelope. He took it out from the pocket of his jeans.

'You can't always have been like this,' Helen wanted to say. 'What happened?'

Instead, she just thanked him again and took it.

He didn't say anything else. He walked her to the door, the ridiculous bulge still there in his trousers, making him hunch a bit and walk funny.

When she waved goodbye, she couldn't tell if he waved back. It was dark in the hall and the door swung closed too quickly.

Even with the lights on, the house is dark. Dark and damp and smelling of wet clothes. Helen's sure this house is what's making her hair go frizzy overnight. She's sure that the house is making her body damp, on the inside. Her heart has drops of condensation on it in the morning. Her lungs have begun to curl like sodden paperbacks.

It's not even fun to live here.

Helen takes her mobile out of her handbag. Two missed calls. Her mum and Duncan. She feels like putting it in the bin.

NO FOOD – is taped to the TV – OR TOILET PAPER. SORRY. USE THE KITCHEN ROLL.

Helen isn't hungry or tired.

She goes upstairs and gets into bed anyway, still in her coat. She puts her sleeve in her mouth and sniffs.

Eventually, a dream comes. Helen is in William's house again, wearing the clothes from the carrier bag. She's putting things on the shelves; a vase with flowers, a framed photograph, a glass figurine of a ballet dancer, a 70p porcelain biscuit jar. She goes into the kitchen and arranges Yorkshire Dales placemats on the table. She pulls a big roll of carpet from her jeans pocket and drapes it over the floorboards.

She is climbing the stairs.

She is hanging curtains.

She is opening the bedroom door.

Then she trips on something. Someone is touching her shoulder and rocking her gently awake. It's dark in the room and at first she thinks it must be Corrine. Helen squints at the person. It's not Corrine. It's the sister.

'What is it?' Helen asks. 'I was sleeping.'

'Come here,' the sister says. 'I want to show you something.'

The sister climbs off the bed and walks over to the wardrobe. She's naked.

'What?' says Helen, pulling the duvet back up over her damp chilly shoulder.

'Come here,' the sister says again.

Helen throws off the covers and gets out of bed, still in her coat and boots, her hair starting to frizz and a tiny drop of cold water sliding down her heart. She goes over to the sister. The sister opens the wardrobe and they look in at Helen's clothes. The sister goes through them, picking out a top, a skirt. She goes over to the dresser, opens a drawer and takes out underwear.

'Are you watching?' the sister says.

'Yep,' Helen says.

The sister puts on the clothes, slowly, one by one, almost sarcastically.

'Okay,' the sister says, once the clothes are on, spinning round on her toes and mimicking a fashion model. 'Who am I?'

Helen doesn't want to speak. She keeps her mouth glued shut.

'Come on. Who am I?'

Helen looks at her. There's nothing else to say.

'You're Helen,' she says.

'That's right,' says the sister. 'Good work. A-star. And who does that make you?'

'I'm Helen, too,' Helen says, knowing how pathetic it sounds.

'You can't have two Helens,' says the sister.

'No,' Helen says, slowly, looking down at her hand, at a small white chink developing in the black nail varnish of her left index finger. 'I suppose not.'

'So?' says the sister.

'I'm an actress,' says Helen. 'I can be whoever I want to be.'

'You're Clair,' says the sister.

'I could be Amanda, Angela or Alice if I wanted,' says Helen. 'Kate, Chloe or Camille.'

'You're Clair,' the sister says, and Clair nods her head.

'Okay,' she says. 'Alright. I'm Clair.'

They sit down on the end of the bed. They have a hug. This is not goodbye. They arrange to keep in touch. 'Put these on,' the sister says, indicating the clothes in the carrier bag.

Clair takes off her black boots and coat and skirt and top and underwear, and puts on the clothes from the future. She goes over to the long mirror and looks at herself in them.

'You look good,' says the sister.

'I do,' says Clair. It's true.

She goes over to the coat. She gets the envelope out and opens it. Inside is five hundred pounds in big red fifty-pound notes. She takes out three hundred, rolls it up and sticks the wad in her hip pocket. She gives the rest to the sister.

'This is for Corrine,' she says. 'For rent.'

'Okay,' says the sister. 'What will you do?'

It's three-something in the morning. Corrine is still out at the casino. Her shift finishes in about an hour.

'I'll be alright,' says Clair. 'I'll be in touch.'

Clair stands outside the house in a borrowed coat of Corrine's, an oversized parka with a furry hood and cuffs. She takes out her mobile, looks at it and doesn't want to call anyone. She puts it back in her pocket.

It would take about half an hour to walk to her mum's house.

It would take about an hour and a half to walk to William's house.

It would take about six days to walk to that farm with the sheep.

Something is tingling in her stomach; a feeling that things will happen, that things will finally happen to her. There's a smell of small, put-out bonfires in the air and the sound of a cat falling off a fence. Things are shining and visible in the sky. She steps out into the street, turns very definitely and starts to walk.

Acknowledgements

Very special thanks to: Charlene Sawit, Steven Hall, Francis Bickmore, Jamie Byng and everyone else at Canongate, my mum and dad, friends, family, and anyone who read an early draft of this novel.

For an even longer thanks list, and other things, please visit: www.thebirdroom.org.uk